ARMAGEDDON—2419 A.D.

Philip Francis Nowlan

HAWK PRESS

Published by

Hawk Press
4836/24, Ansari Road, Daryaganj
New Delhi – 110 002
Phones : 9643330713, +91-11-23278618, +91-11-35676207
E-mail: thehawkpress@gmail.com
www.thehawkpress.com

ISBN : 978-93-92322-75-4

Contents

Foreword

ELSEWHERE I have set down, for whatever interest they have in this, the 25th Century, my personal recollections of the 20th Century.

Now it occurs to me that my memoirs of the 25th Century may have an equal interest 500 years from now—particularly in view of that unique perspective from which I have seen the 25th Century, entering it as I did, in one leap across a gap of 492 years.

This statement requires elucidation. There are still many in the world who are not familiar with my unique experience. Five centuries from now there may be many more, especially if civilization is fated to endure any worse convulsions than those which have occurred between 1975 A.D. and the present time.

I should state therefore, that I, Anthony Rogers, am, so far as I know, the only man alive whose normal span of eighty-one years of life has been spread over a period of 573 years. To be precise, I lived the first twenty-nine years of my life between 1898 and 1927; the other fifty-two since 2419. The gap between these two, a period of nearly five hundred years, I spent in a state of suspended animation, free from the ravages of katabolic processes, and without any apparent effect on my physical or mental faculties.

When I began my long sleep, man had just begun his real conquest of the air in a sudden series of transoceanic flights in airplanes driven by internal combustion motors. He had barely begun to speculate on the possibilities of harnessing sub-atomic forces, and had made no further practical penetration into the field of ethereal pulsations than the primitive radio and television of that day. The United States of America was the most powerful nation in the world, its political, financial, industrial and scientific influence being supreme; and in the arts also it was rapidly climbing into leadership.

I awoke to find the America I knew a total wreck—to find Americans a hunted race in their own land, hiding in the dense forests that covered the shattered and leveled ruins of their once magnificent cities, desperately preserving, and struggling to develop in their secret retreats, the remnants of their culture and science—and the undying flame of their sturdy independence.

World domination was in the hands of Mongolians and the center of world power lay in inland China, with Americans one of the few races of mankind unsubdued—and it must be admitted in fairness to the truth, not worth the trouble of subduing in the eyes of the Han Airlords who ruled North America as titular tributaries of the Most Magnificent.

For they needed not the forests in which the Americans lived, nor the resources of the vast territories these forests covered. With the perfection to which they had reduced the synthetic production of necessities and luxuries, their remarkable development of scientific processes and mechanical accomplishment of work, they had no economic need for the forests, and no economic desire for the enslaved labor of an unruly race.

They had all they needed for their magnificently luxurious and degraded scheme of civilization, within the walls of the fifteen cities of sparkling glass they had flung skyward on the sites of ancient American centers, into the bowels of the earth underneath them, and with relatively small surrounding areas of agriculture.

Complete domination of the air rendered communication between these centers a matter of ease and safety. Occasional destructive raids on the waste lands were considered all that was necessary to keep the "wild" Americans on the run within the shelter of their forests, and prevent their becoming a menace to the Han civilization.

But nearly three hundred years of easily maintained security, the last century of which had been nearly sterile in scientific, social and economic progress, had softened and devitalized the Hans.

It had likewise developed, beneath the protecting foliage of the forest, the growth of a vigorous new American civilization, remarkable in the mobility and flexibility of its organization, in its conquest of almost insuperable obstacles, in the development and guarding of its industrial and scientific resources, all in anticipation of that "Day of

Hope" to which it had been looking forward for generations, when it would be strong enough to burst from the green chrysalis of the forests, soar into the upper air lanes and destroy the yellow incubus.

At the time I awoke, the "Day of Hope" was almost at hand. I shall not attempt to set forth a detailed history of the Second War of Independence, for that has been recorded already by better historians than I am. Instead I shall confine myself largely to the part I was fortunate enough to play in this struggle and in the events leading up to it.

It all resulted from my interest in radioactive gases. During the latter part of 1927 my company, the American Radioactive Gas Corporation, had been keeping me busy investigating reports of unusual phenomena observed in certain abandoned coal mines near the Wyoming Valley, in Pennsylvania.

With two assistants and a complete equipment of scientific instruments, I began the exploration of a deserted working in a mountainous district, where several weeks before, a number of mining engineers had reported traces of carnotite[1] and what they believed to be radioactive gases. Their report was not without foundation, it was apparent from the outset, for in our examination of the upper levels of the mine, our instruments indicated a vigorous radioactivity.

[1] A hydrovanadate of uranium, and other metals; used as a source of radium compounds.

On the morning of December 15th, we descended to one of the lowest levels. To our surprise, we found no water there. Obviously it had drained off through some break in the strata. We noticed too that the rock in the side walls of the shaft was soft, evidently due to the radioactivity, and pieces crumbled under foot rather easily. We made our way cautiously down the shaft, when suddenly the rotted timbers above us gave way.

I jumped ahead, barely escaping the avalanche of coal and soft rock, but my companions, who were several paces behind me, were buried under it, and undoubtedly met instant death.

I was trapped. Return was impossible. With my electric torch I explored the shaft to its end, but could find no other way out. The air became increasingly difficult to breathe, probably from the rapid accumulation of the radioactive gas. In a little while my senses reeled and I lost consciousness.

When I awoke, there was a cool and refreshing circulation of air in the shaft. I had no thought that I had been unconscious more than a few hours, although it seems that the radioactive gas had kept me in a state of suspended animation for something like 500 years. My awakening, I figured out later, had been due to some shifting of the strata which reopened the shaft and cleared the atmosphere in the working. This must have been the case, for I was able to struggle back up the shaft over a pile of debris, and stagger up the long incline to the mouth of the mine, where an entirely different world, overgrown with a vast forest and no visible sign of human habitation, met my eyes.

I shall pass over the days of mental agony that followed in my attempt to grasp the meaning of it all. There were times when I felt that I was on the verge of insanity. I roamed the unfamiliar forest like a lost soul. Had it not been for the necessity of improvising traps and crude clubs with which to slay my food, I believe I should have gone mad.

Suffice it to say, however, that I survived this psychic crisis. I shall begin my narrative proper with my first contact with Americans of the year 2419 A.D.

Chapter I.

Floating Men

My first glimpse of a human being of the 25th Century was obtained through a portion of woodland where the trees were thinly scattered, with a dense forest beyond.

I had been wandering along aimlessly, and hopelessly, musing over my strange fate, when I noticed a figure that cautiously backed out of the dense growth across the glade. I was about to call out joyfully, but there was something furtive about the figure that prevented me. The boy's attention (for it seemed to be a lad of fifteen or sixteen) was centered tensely on the heavy growth of trees from which he had just emerged.

He was clad in rather tight-fitting garments entirely of green, and wore a helmet-like cap of the same color. High around his waist he wore a broad, thick belt, which bulked up in the back across the shoulders, into something of the proportions of a knapsack.

As I was taking in these details, there came a vivid flash and heavy detonation, like that of a hand grenade, not far to the left of him. He threw up an arm and staggered a bit in a queer, gliding way; then he recovered himself and slipped cautiously away from the place of the explosion, crouching slightly, and still facing the denser part of the forest. Every few steps he would raise his arm, and point into the forest with something he held in his hand. Wherever he pointed there was a terrific explosion, deeper in among the trees. It came to me then that he was shooting with some form of pistol, though there was neither flash nor detonation from the muzzle of the weapon itself.

After firing several times, he seemed to come to a sudden resolution, and turning in my general direction, leaped—to my amazement sailing through the air between the sparsely scattered trees in such a jump as I had never in my life seen before. That leap must have carried him a full fifty feet, although at the height of his arc, he was not more than ten or twelve feet from the ground.

When he alighted, his foot caught in a projecting root, and he sprawled gently forward. I say "gently" for he did not crash down as I expected him to do. The only thing I could compare it with was a slow-motion cinema, although I had never seen one in which horizontal motions were registered at normal speed and only the vertical movements were slowed down.

Seen upon the ultroscope viewplate, the battle looked as though it were being fought in daylight, perhaps on a cloudy day, while the explosions of the rockets appeared as flashes of extra brilliance.

Due to my surprise, I suppose my brain did not function with its normal quickness, for I gazed at the prone figure for several seconds before I saw the blood that oozed out from under the tight green cap. Regaining my power of action, I dragged him out of sight back of the big tree. For a few moments I busied myself in an attempt to staunch the flow of blood. The wound was not a deep one. My companion was more dazed than hurt. But what of the pursuers?

I took the weapon from his grasp and examined it hurriedly. It was not unlike the automatic pistol to which I was accustomed, except that it apparently fired with a button instead of a trigger. I inserted several fresh rounds of ammunition into its magazine from my companion's belt, as rapidly as I could, for I soon heard, near us, the suppressed conversation of his pursuers.

There followed a series of explosions round about us, but none very close. They evidently had not spotted our hiding place, and were firing at random.

I waited tensely, balancing the gun in my hand, to accustom myself to its weight and probable throw.

Then I saw a movement in the green foliage of a tree not far away, and the head and face of a man appeared. Like my companion, he was clad entirely in green, which made his figure difficult to distinguish. But his face could be seen clearly. It was an evil face, and had murder in it.

That decided me. I raised the gun and fired. My aim was bad, for there was no kick in the gun, as I had expected, and I hit the trunk of the tree several feet below him. It blew him from his perch like a crumpled bit of paper, and he floated down to the ground, like some limp, dead thing, gently lowered by an invisible hand. The tree, its trunk blown apart by the explosion, crashed down.

There followed another series of explosions around us. These guns we were using made no sound in the firing, and my opponents were evidently as much at sea as to my position as I was to theirs. So I made no attempt to reply to their fire, contenting myself with keeping a sharp lookout in their general direction. And patience had its reward.

Very soon I saw a cautious movement in the top of another tree. Exposing myself as little as possible, I aimed carefully at the tree trunk and fired again. A shriek followed the explosion. I heard the tree crash down; then a groan.

There was silence for a while. Then I heard a faint sound of boughs swishing. I shot three times in its direction, pressing the button as rapidly as I could. Branches crashed down where my shells had exploded, but there was no body.

Then I saw one of them. He was starting one of those amazing leaps from the bough of one tree to another, about forty feet away.

I threw up my gun impulsively and fired. By now I had gotten the feel of the weapon, and my aim was good. I hit him. The "bullet" must have penetrated his body and exploded. For one moment I saw him flying through the air. Then the explosion, and he had vanished. He never finished his leap. It was annihilation.

How many more of them there were I don't know. But this must have been too much for them. They used a final round of shells on us, all of which exploded harmlessly, and shortly after I heard them swishing and crashing away from us through the tree tops. Not one of them descended to earth.

Now I had time to give some attention to my companion. She was, I found, a girl, and not a boy. Despite her bulky appearance, due to the peculiar belt strapped around her body high up under the arms, she was very slender, and very pretty.

There was a stream not far away, from which I brought water and bathed her face and wound.

Apparently the mystery of these long leaps, the monkey-like ability to jump from bough to bough, and of the bodies that floated gently down instead of falling, lay in the belt. The thing was some sort of anti-gravity belt that almost balanced the weight of the wearer, thereby tremendously multiplying the propulsive power of the leg muscles, and the lifting power of the arms.

When the girl came to, she regarded me as curiously as I did her, and promptly began to quiz me. Her accent and intonation puzzled me a lot, but nevertheless we were able to understand each other fairly well, except for certain words and phrases. I explained what had happened while she lay unconscious, and she thanked me simply for saving her life.

"You are a strange exchange," she said, eying my clothing quizzically. Evidently she found it mirth provoking by contrast with her own neatly efficient garb. "Don't you understand what I mean by 'exchange?' I mean ah—let me see—a stranger, somebody from some other gang. What gang do you belong to?" (She pronounced it "gan," with only a suspicion of a nasal sound.)

I laughed. "I'm not a gangster," I said. But she evidently did not understand this word. "I don't belong to any gang," I explained, "and never did. Does everybody belong to a gang nowadays?"

"Naturally," she said, frowning. "If you don't belong to a gang, where and how do you live? Why have you not found and joined a gang? How do you eat? Where do you get your clothing?"

"I've been eating wild game for the past two weeks," I explained, "and this clothing I—er—ah—." I paused, wondering how I could explain that it must be many hundred years old.

In the end I saw I would have to tell my story as well as I could, piecing it together with my assumptions as to what had happened. She listened patiently; incredulously at first, but with more confidence as I went on. When I had finished, she sat thinking for a long time.

"That's hard to believe," she said, "but I believe it." She looked me over with frank interest.

"Were you married when you slipped into unconsciousness down in that mine?" she asked me suddenly. I assured her I had never married. "Well, that simplifies matters," she continued. "You see, if you were technically classed as a family man, I could take you back only as an invited exchange and I, being unmarried, and no relation of yours, couldn't do the inviting."

Chapter II.

The Forest Gangs

She gave me a brief outline of the very peculiar social and economic system under which her people lived. At least it seemed very peculiar from my 20th Century viewpoint.

I learned with amazement that exactly 492 years had passed over my head as I lay unconscious in the mine.

Wilma, for that was her name, did not profess to be a historian, and so could give me only a sketchy outline of the wars that had been fought, and the manner in which such radical changes had come about. It seemed that another war had followed the First World War, in which nearly all the European nations had banded together to break the financial and industrial power of America. They succeeded in their purpose, though they were beaten, for the war was a terrific one, and left America, like themselves, gasping, bleeding and disorganized, with only the hollow shell of a victory.

This opportunity had been seized by the Russian Soviets, who had made a coalition with the Chinese, to sweep over all Europe and reduce it to a state of chaos.

America, industrially geared to world production and the world trade, collapsed economically, and there ensued a long period of stagnation and desperate attempts at economic reconstruction. But it was impossible to stave off war with the Mongolians, who by now had subjugated the Russians, and were aiming at a world empire.

In about 2109, it seems, the conflict was finally precipitated. The Mongolians, with overwhelming fleets of great airships, and a science that far outstripped that of crippled America, swept in over the Pacific and Atlantic Coasts, and down from Canada, annihilating American aircraft, armies and cities with their terrific disintegrator rays. These rays were projected from a machine not unlike a searchlight in appearance, the reflector of which, however, was not material substance, but a complicated balance of interacting electronic forces. This resulted in a terribly destructive beam. Under its influence, material substance melted into "nothingness"; i. e., into electronic vibrations. It destroyed all then known substances, from air to the most dense metals and stone.

They settled down to the establishment of what became known as the Han dynasty in America, as a sort of province in their World Empire.

Those were terrible days for the Americans. They were hunted like wild beasts. Only those survived who finally found refuge in mountains, canyons and forests. Government was at an end among them. Anarchy prevailed for several generations. Most would have been eager to submit to the Hans, even if it meant slavery. But the Hans did not want them, for they themselves had marvelous machinery and scientific process by which all difficult labor was accomplished.

Ultimately they stopped their active search for, and annihilation of, the widely scattered groups of now savage Americans. So long as they remained hidden in their forests, and did not venture near the great cities the Hans had built, little attention was paid to them.

Then began the building of the new American civilization. Families and individuals gathered together in clans or "gangs" for mutual protection. For nearly a century they lived a nomadic and primitive life, moving from place to place, in desperate fear of the casual and occasional Han air raids, and the terrible disintegrator ray. As the frequency of these raids decreased, they began to stay permanently in given localities, organizing upon lines which in many respects were similar to those of the military households of the Norman feudal barons, except that instead of gathering together in castles, their defense tactics necessitated a certain scattering of living quarters for families and individuals. They lived virtually in the open air, in the forests, in green tents, resorting to camouflage tactics that would conceal their presence from air observers. They dug underground factories and laboratories, that they might better be shielded from the electrical detectors of the Hans. They tapped the radio communication lines of the Hans, with crude instruments at first;

better ones later on. They bent every effort toward the redevelopment of science. For many generations they labored as unseen, unknown scholars of the Hans, picking up their knowledge piecemeal, as fast as they were able to.

During the earlier part of this period, there were many deadly wars fought between the various gangs, and occasional courageous but childishly futile attacks upon the Hans, followed by terribly punitive raids.

But as knowledge progressed, the sense of American brotherhood redeveloped. Reciprocal arrangements were made among the gangs over constantly increasing areas. Trade developed to a certain extent, as between one gang and another. But the interchange of knowledge became more important than that of goods, as skill in the handling of synthetic processes developed.

Within the gang, an economy was developed that was a compromise between individual liberty and a military socialism. The right of private property was limited practically to personal possessions, but private privileges were many, and sacredly regarded. Stimulation to achievement lay chiefly in the winning of various kinds of leadership and prerogatives, and only in a very limited degree in the hope of owning anything that might be classified as "wealth," and nothing that might be classified as "resources." Resources of every description, for military safety and efficiency, belonged as a matter of public interest to the community as a whole.

In the meantime, through these many generations, the Hans had developed a luxury economy, and with it the perfection of gilded vice and degradation. The Americans were regarded as "wild men of the woods." And since they neither needed nor wanted the woods or the wild men, they treated them as beasts, and were conscious of no human brotherhood with them. As time went on, and synthetic processes of producing foods and materials were further developed, less and less ground was needed by the Hans for the purposes of agriculture, and finally, even the working of mines was abandoned when it became cheaper to build up metal from electronic vibrations than to dig them out of the ground.

The Han race, devitalized by its vices and luxuries, with machinery and scientific processes to satisfy its every want, with virtually no necessity of labor, began to assume a defensive attitude toward the Americans.

And quite naturally, the Americans regarded the Hans with a deep, grim hatred. Conscious of individual superiority as men, knowing that latterly they were outstripping the Hans in science and civilization, they longed desperately for the day when they should be powerful enough to rise and annihilate the Yellow Blight that lay over the continent.

At the time of my awakening, the gangs were rather loosely organized, but were considering the establishment of a special military force, whose special business it would be to harry the Hans and bring down their air ships whenever possible without causing general alarm among the Mongolians. This force was destined to become the nucleus of the national force, when the Day of Retribution arrived. But that, however, did not happen for ten years, and is another story.

Wilma told me she was a member of the Wyoming Gang, which claimed the entire Wyoming Valley as its territory, under the leadership of Boss Hart. Her mother and father were dead, and she was unmarried, so she was not a "family member." She lived in a little group of tents known as Camp 17, under a woman Camp Boss, with seven other girls.

Her duties alternated between military or police scouting and factory work. For the two-week period which would end the next day, she had been on "air patrol." This did not mean, as I first imagined, that she was flying, but rather that she was on the lookout for Han ships over this outlying section of the Wyoming territory, and had spent most of her time perched in the tree tops scanning the skies. Had she seen one she would have fired a "drop flare" several miles off to one side, which would ignite when it was floating vertically toward the earth, so that the direction or point from which it had been fired might not be guessed by the airship and bring a blasting play of the disintegrator ray in her vicinity. Other members of the air patrol would send up rockets on seeing hers, until finally a scout equipped with an ultrophone, which, unlike the ancient radio, operated on the ultronic ethereal vibrations, would pass the warning simultaneously to the headquarters of the Wyoming Gang and other communities within a radius of several hundred miles, not to mention the few American rocket ships that might be in the air, and which instantly would duck to cover either through forest clearings or by flattening down to earth in green fields where their coloring would probably protect them from observation. The favorite American method of propulsion was known as "rocketing." The rocket is what I would describe, from my 20th Century comprehension of the matter, as an extremely powerful gas blast, atomically produced through the stimulation of chemical action. Scientists of today regard it as a childishly simple reaction, but by that very virtue, most economical and efficient.

On the left of the illustration is a Han girl, and on the right is an American girl, who, like all of her race, is equipped with an inertron belt and a rocket gun.

But tomorrow, she explained, she would go back to work in the cloth plant, where she would take charge of one of the synthetic processes by which those wonderful substitutes for woven fabrics of wool, cotton and silk are produced. At the end of another two weeks, she would be back on military duty again, perhaps at the same work, or maybe as a "contact guard," on duty where the territory of the Wyomings merged with that of the Delawares, or the "Susquannas" (Susquehannas) or one of the half dozen other "gangs" in that section of the country which I knew as Pennsylvania and New York States.

Wilma cleared up for me the mystery of those flying leaps which she and her assailants had made, and explained in the following manner, how the inertron belt balances weight:

"Jumpers" were in common use at the time I "awoke," though they were costly, for at that time inertron had not been produced in very great quantity. They were very useful in the forest. They were belts, strapped high under the arms, containing an amount of inertron adjusted to the wearer's weight and purposes. In effect they made a man weigh as little as he desired; two pounds if he liked.

"Floaters" are a later development of "jumpers"—rocket motors encased in inertron blocks and strapped to the back in such a way that the wearer floats, when drifting, facing slightly downward. With his motor in operation, he moves like a diver, headforemost, controlling his direction by twisting his body and by movements of his outstretched arms and hands. Ballast weights locked in the front of the belt adjust weight and lift. Some men prefer a few ounces of weight in floating, using a slight motor thrust to overcome this. Others prefer a buoyance balance of a few ounces. The inadvertent dropping of weight is not a serious matter. The motor thrust always can be used to descend. But as an extra precaution, in case the motor should fail, for any reason, there are built into every belt a number of detachable sections, one or more of which can be discarded to balance off any loss in weight.

"But who were your assailants," I asked, "and why were you attacked?"

Her assailants, she told me, were members of an outlaw gang, referred to as "Bad Bloods," a group which for several generations had been under the domination of conscienceless leaders who tried to advance the interests of their clan by tactics which their neighbors had come to regard as unfair, and who in consequence had been virtually boycotted. Their purpose had been to slay her near the Delaware frontier, making it appear that the crime had been committed by Delaware scouts and thus embroil the Delawares and Wyomings in acts of reprisal against each other, or at least cause suspicions.

Fortunately they had not succeeded in surprising her, and she had been successful in dodging them for some two hours before the shooting began, at the moment when I arrived on the scene.

"But we must not stay here talking," Wilma concluded. "I have to take you in, and besides I must report this attack right away. I think we had better slip over to the other side of the mountain. Whoever is on that post will have a phone, and I can make a direct report. But you'll have to have a belt. Mine alone won't help much against our combined weights, and there's little to be gained by jumping heavy. It's almost as bad as walking."

After a little search, we found one of the men I had killed, who had floated down among the trees some distance away and whose belt was not badly damaged. In detaching it from his body, it nearly got away from me and shot up in the air. Wilma caught it, however, and though it reinforced the lift of her own belt so that she had to hook her knee around a branch to hold herself down, she saved it. I climbed the tree and, with my weight added to hers, we floated down easily.

Chapter III.
Life in the 25th Century

We were delayed in starting for quite a while since I had to acquire a few crude ideas about the technique of using these belts. I had been sitting down, for instance, with the belt strapped about me, enjoying an ease similar to that of a comfortable armchair; when I stood up with a natural exertion of muscular effort, I shot ten feet into the air, with a wild instinctive thrashing of arms and legs that amused Wilma greatly.

But after some practice, I began to get the trick of gauging muscular effort to a minimum of vertical and a maximum of horizontal. The correct form, I found, was in a measure comparable to that of skating. I found, also, that in forest work particularly the arms and hands could be used to great advantage in swinging along from branch to branch, so prolonging leaps almost indefinitely at times.

In going up the side of the mountain, I found that my 20th Century muscles did have an advantage, in spite of lack of skill with the belt, and since the slopes were very sharp, and most of our leaps were upward, I could have distanced Wilma easily. But when we crossed the ridge and descended, she outstripped me with her superior technique. Choosing the steepest slopes, she would crouch in the top of a tree, and propel herself outward, literally diving until, with the loss of horizontal momentum, she would assume a more upright position and float downward. In this manner she would sometimes cover as much as a quarter of a mile in a single leap, while I leaped and scrambled clumsily behind, thoroughly enjoying the novel sensation.

Half way down the mountain, we saw another green-clad figure leap out above the tree tops toward us. The three of us perched on an outcropping of rock from which a view for many miles around could be had, while Wilma hastily explained her adventure and my presence to her fellow guard; whose name was Alan. I learned later that this was the modern form of Helen.

"You want to report by phone then, don't you?" Alan took a compact packet about six inches square from a holster attached to her belt and handed it to Wilma.

So far as I could see, it had no special receiver for the ear. Wilma merely threw back a lid, as though she were opening a book, and began to talk. The voice that came back from the machine was as audible as her own.

She was queried closely as to the attack upon her, and at considerable length as to myself, and I could tell from the tone of that voice that its owner was not prepared to take me at my face value as readily as Wilma had. For that matter, neither was the other girl. I could realize it from the suspicious glances she threw my way, when she thought my attention was elsewhere, and the manner in which her hand hovered constantly near her gun holster.

Wilma was ordered to bring me in at once, and informed that another scout would take her place on the other side of the mountain. So she closed down the lid of the phone and handed it back to Alan, who seemed relieved to see us departing over the tree tops in the direction of the camps.

We had covered perhaps ten miles, in what still seemed to me a surprisingly easy fashion, when Wilma explained, that from here on we would have to keep to the ground. We were nearing the camps, she said, and there was always the possibility that some small Han scoutship, invisible high in the sky, might catch sight of us through a projectoscope and thus find the general location of the camps.

Wilma took me to the Scout office, which proved to be a small building of irregular shape, conforming to the trees around it, and substantially constructed of green sheet-like material.

I was received by the assistant Scout Boss, who reported my arrival at once to the historical office, and to officials he called the Psycho Boss and the History Boss, who came in a few minutes later. The attitude of all three men was at first polite but skeptical, and Wilma's ardent advocacy seemed to amuse them secretly.

For the next two hours I talked, explained and answered questions. I had to explain, in detail, the manner of my life in the 20th Century and my understanding of customs, habits, business, science and the history of that period, and about developments in the centuries that had elapsed. Had I been in a classroom, I would have come through the examination with a very poor mark, for I was unable to give any answer to fully half of their questions. But before long I realized that the majority of these questions were designed as traps. Objects, of whose purpose I knew nothing, were casually handed to me, and I was watched keenly as I handled them.

In the end I could see both amazement and belief begin to show in the faces of my inquisitors, and at last the Historical and Psycho Bosses agreed openly that they could find no flaw in my story or reactions, and that unbelievable as it seemed, my story must be accepted as genuine.

They took me at once to Big Boss Hart. He was a portly man with a "poker face." He would probably have been the successful politician even in the 20th Century.

They gave him a brief outline of my story and a report of their examination of me. He made no comment other than to nod his acceptance of it. Then he turned to me.

"How does it feel?" he asked. "Do we look funny to you?"

"A bit strange," I admitted. "But I'm beginning to lose that dazed feeling, though I can see I have an awful lot to learn."

"Maybe we can learn some things from you, too," he said. "So you fought in the First World War. Do you know, we have very little left in the way of records of the details of that war, that is, the precise conditions under which it was fought, and the tactics employed. We forgot many things during the Han terror, and—well, I think you might have a lot of ideas worth thinking over for our raid masters. By the way, now that you're here, and can't go back to your own century, so to speak, what do you want to do? You're welcome to become one of us. Or perhaps you'd just like to visit with us for a while, and then look around among the other gangs. Maybe you'd like some of the others better. Don't make up your mind now. We'll put you down as an exchange for a while. Let's see. You and Bill Hearn ought to get along well together. He's Camp Boss of Number 34 when he isn't acting as Raid Boss or Scout Boss. There's a vacancy in his camp. Stay with him and think things over as long as you want to. As soon as you make up your mind to anything, let me know."

We all shook hands, for that was one custom that had not died out in five hundred years, and I set out with Bill Hearn.

Bill, like all the others, was clad in green. He was a big man. That is, he was about my own height, five feet eleven. This was considerably above the average now, for the race had lost something in stature, it seemed, through the vicissitudes of five centuries. Most of the women were a bit below five feet, and the men only a trifle above this height.

For a period of two weeks Bill was to confine himself to camp duties, so I had a good chance to familiarize myself with the community life. It was not easy. There were so many marvels to absorb. I never ceased to wonder at the strange combination of rustic social life and feverish industrial activity. At least, it was strange to me. For in my experience, industrial development meant crowded cities, tenements, paved streets, profusion of vehicles, noise, hurrying men and women with strained or dull faces, vast structures and ornate public works.

Here, however, was rustic simplicity, apparently isolated families and groups, living in the heart of the forest, with a quarter of a mile or more between households, a total absence of crowds, no means of conveyance other than the belts called jumpers, almost constantly worn by everybody, and an occasional rocket ship, used only for longer journeys, and underground plants or factories that were to my mind more like laboratories and engine rooms; many of them were excavations as deep as mines, with well finished, lighted and comfortable interiors. These people were adepts at camouflage against air observation. Not only would their activity have been unsuspected by an airship passing over the center of the community, but even by an enemy who might happen to drop through the screen of the upper branches to the floor of the forest. The camps, or household structures, were all irregular in shape and of colors that blended with the great trees among which they were hidden.

There were 724 dwellings or "camps" among the Wyomings, located within an area of about fifteen square miles. The total population was 8,688, every man, woman and child, whether member or "exchange," being listed.

The plants were widely scattered through the territory also. Nowhere was anything like congestion permitted. So far as possible, families and individuals were assigned to living quarters, not too far from the plants or offices in which their work lay.

All able-bodied men and women alternated in two-week periods between military and industrial service, except those who were needed for household work. Since working conditions in the plants and offices were ideal, and everybody thus had plenty of healthy outdoor activity in addition, the population was sturdy and active. Laziness was regarded as nearly the greatest of social offenses. Hard work and general merit were variously rewarded with extra privileges, advancement to positions of authority, and with various items of personal equipment for convenience and luxury.

In leisure moments, I got great enjoyment from sitting outside the dwelling in which I was quartered with Bill Hearn and ten other men, watching the occasional passers-by, as with leisurely, but swift movements, they swung up and down the forest trail, rising from the ground in long almost-horizontal leaps, occasionally swinging from one convenient branch overhead to another before "sliding" back to the ground farther on. Normal traveling pace, where these trails were straight enough, was about twenty miles an hour. Such things as automobiles and railroad trains (the memory of them not more than a month old in my mind) seemed inexpressibly silly and futile compared with such convenience as these belts or jumpers offered.

Bill suggested that I wander around for several days, from plant to plant, to observe and study what I could. The entire community had been apprised of my coming, my rating as an "exchange" reaching every building and post in the community, by means of ultronic broadcast. Everywhere I was welcomed in an interested and helpful spirit.

I visited the plants where ultronic vibrations were isolated from the ether and through slow processes built up into sub-electronic, electronic and atomic forms into the two great synthetic elements, ultron and inertron. I learned something, superficially at least, of the processes of combined chemical and mechanical action through which were produced the various forms of synthetic cloth. I watched the manufacture of the machines which were used at locations of construction to produce the various forms of building materials. But I was particularly interested in the munitions plants and the rocket-ship shops.

Ultron is a solid of great molecular density and moderate elasticity, which has the property of being 100 percent conductive to those pulsations known as light, electricity and heat. Since it is completely permeable to light vibrations, it is therefore absolutely invisible and non-reflective. Its magnetic response is almost, but not quite, 100 percent also. It is therefore very heavy under normal conditions but extremely responsive to the repellor or anti-gravity rays, such as the Hans use as "legs" for their airships.

Inertron is the second great triumph of American research and experimentation with ultronic forces. It was developed just a few years before my awakening in the abandoned mine. It is a synthetic element, built up, through a complicated heterodyning of ultronic pulsations, from "infra-balanced" sub-ionic forms. It is completely inert to both electric and magnetic forces in all the orders above the ultronic; that is to say, the sub-electronic, the electronic, the atomic and the molecular. In consequence it has a number of amazing and valuable properties. One of these is the total lack of weight. Another is a total lack of heat. It has no molecular vibration whatever. It reflects 100 percent of the heat and light impinging upon it. It does not feel cold to the touch, of course, since it will not absorb the heat of the hand. It is a solid, very dense in molecular structure despite its lack of weight, of great strength and considerable elasticity. It is a perfect shield against the disintegrator rays.

Rocket guns are very simple contrivances so far as the mechanism of launching the bullet is concerned. They are simple light tubes, closed at the rear end, with a trigger-actuated pin for piercing the thin skin at the base of the cartridge. This piercing of the skin starts the chemical and atomic reaction. The entire cartridge leaves the tube under its own power, at a very easy initial velocity, just enough to insure accuracy of aim; so the tube does not have to be of heavy construction. The bullet increases in velocity as it goes. It may be solid or explosive. It may explode on contact or on time, or a combination of these two.

Setting his rocket gun for a long-distance shot.

Bill and I talked mostly of weapons, military tactics and strategy. Strangely enough he had no idea whatever of the possibilities of the barrage, though the tremendous effect of a "curtain of fire" with such high-explosive projectiles as these modern rocket guns used was obvious to me. But the barrage idea, it seemed, has been lost track of completely in the air wars that followed the First World War, and in the peculiar guerilla tactics developed by Americans in the later period of operations from the ground against Han airships, and in the gang wars which, until a few generations ago I learned, had been almost continuous.

"I wonder," said Bill one day, "if we couldn't work up some form of barrage to spring on the Bad Bloods. The Big Boss told me today that he's been in communication with the other gangs, and all are agreed that the Bad Bloods might as well be wiped out for good. That attempt on Wilma Deering's life and their evident desire to make trouble among the gangs, has stirred up every community east of the Alleghenies. The Boss says that none of the others will object if we go after them. So I imagine that before long we will. Now show me again how you worked that business in the Argonne forest. The conditions ought to be pretty much the same."

I went over it with him in detail, and gradually we worked out a modified plan that would be better adapted to our more powerful weapons, and the use of jumpers.

"It will be easy," Bill exulted. "I'll slide down and talk it over with the Boss tomorrow."

During the first two weeks of my stay with the Wyomings, Wilma Deering and I saw a great deal of each other. I naturally felt a little closer friendship for her, in view of the fact that she was the first human being I saw after waking from my long sleep; her appreciation of my saving her life, though I could not have done otherwise than I did in that matter, and most of all my own appreciation of the fact that she had not found it as difficult as the others to believe my story, operated in the same direction. I could easily imagine my story must have sounded incredible.

It was natural enough too, that she should feel an unusual interest in me. In the first place, I was her personal discovery. In the second, she was a girl of studious and reflective turn of mind. She never got tired of my stories and descriptions of the 20th Century.

The others of the community, however, seemed to find our friendship a bit amusing. It seemed that Wilma had a reputation for being cold toward the opposite sex, and so others, not being able to appreciate some of her fine qualities as I did, misinterpreted her attitude, much to their own delight. Wilma and I, however, ignored this as much as we could.

Chapter IV.
A Han Air Raid

There was a girl in Wilma's camp named Gerdi Mann, with whom Bill Hearn was desperately in love, and the four of us used to go around a lot together. Gerdi was a distinct type. Whereas Wilma had the usual dark brown hair and hazel eyes that marked nearly every member of the community, Gerdi had red hair, blue eyes and very fair skin. She has been dead many years now, but I remember her vividly because she was a throwback in physical appearance to a certain 20th Century type which I have found very rare among modern Americans; also because the four of us were engaged one day in a discussion of this very point, when I obtained my first experience of a Han air raid.

We were sitting high on the side of a hill overlooking the valley that teemed with human activity, invisible beneath its blanket of foliage.

The other three, who knew of the Irish but vaguely and indefinitely, as a race on the other side of the globe, which, like ourselves, had succeeded in maintaining a precarious and fugitive existence in rebellion against the Mongolian domination of the earth, were listening with interest to my theory that Gerdi's ancestors of several hundred years ago must have been Irish. I explained that Gerdi was an Irish type, evidently a throwback, and that her surname might well have been McMann, or McMahan, and still more anciently "mac Mathghamhain." They were interested too in my surmise that "Gerdi" was the same name as that which had been "Gerty" or "Gertrude" in the 20th Century.

In the middle of our discussion, we were startled by an alarm rocket that burst high in the air, far to the north, spreading a pall of red smoke that drifted like a cloud. It was followed by others at scattered points in the northern sky.

"A Han raid!" Bill exclaimed in amazement. "The first in seven years!"

"Maybe it's just one of their ships off its course," I ventured.

"No," said Wilma in some agitation. "That would be green rockets. Red means only one thing, Tony. They're sweeping the countryside with their dis beams. Can you see anything, Bill?"

"We had better get under cover," Gerdi said nervously. "The four of us are bunched here in the open. For all we know they may be twelve miles up, out of sight, yet looking at us with a projecto'."

Bill had been sweeping the horizon hastily with his glass, but apparently saw nothing.

"We had better scatter, at that," he said finally. "It's orders, you know. See!" He pointed to the valley.

Here and there a tiny human figure shot for a moment above the foliage of the treetops.

"That's bad," Wilma commented, as she counted the jumpers. "No less than fifteen people visible, and all clearly radiating from a central point. Do they want to give away our location?"

The standard orders covering air raids were that the population was to scatter individually. There should be no grouping, or even pairing, in view of the destructiveness of the disintegrator rays. Experience of generations had proved that if this were done, and everybody remained hidden beneath the tree screens, the Hans would have to sweep mile after mile of territory, foot by foot, to catch more than a small percentage of the community.

Gerdi, however, refused to leave Bill, and Wilma developed an equal obstinacy against quitting my side. I was inexperienced at this sort of thing, she explained, quite ignoring the fact that she was too; she was only thirteen or fourteen years old at the time of the last air raid.

However, since I could not argue her out of it, we leaped together about a quarter of a mile to the right, while Bill and Gerdi disappeared down the hillside among the trees.

Wilma and I both wanted a point of vantage from which we might overlook the valley and the sky to the north, and we found it near the top of the ridge, where, protected from visibility by thick branches, we could look out between the tree trunks, and get a good view of the valley.

No more rockets went up. Except for a few of those warning red clouds, drifting lazily in a blue sky, there was no visible indication of man's past or present existence anywhere in the sky or on the ground.

Then Wilma gripped my arm and pointed. I saw it; away off in the distance; looking like a phantom dirigible airship, in its coat of low-visibility paint, a bare spectre.

"Seven thousand feet up," Wilma whispered, crouching close to me. "Watch."

The ship was about the same shape as the great dirigibles of the 20th Century that I had seen, but without the suspended control car, engines, propellors, rudders or elevating planes. As it loomed rapidly nearer, I saw that it was wider and somewhat flatter than I had supposed.

Now I could see the repellor rays that held the ship aloft, like searchlight beams faintly visible in the bright daylight (and still faintly visible to the human eye at night). Actually, I had been informed by my instructors, there were two rays; the visible one generated by the ship's apparatus, and directed toward the ground as a beam of "carrier" impulses; and the true repellor ray, the complement of the other in one sense, induced by the action of the "carrier" and reacting in a concentrating upward direction from the mass of the earth, becoming successively electronic, atomic and finally molecular, in its nature, according to various ratios of distance between earth mass and "carrier" source, until, in the last analysis, the ship itself actually is supported on an upward rushing column of air, much like a ball continuously supported on a fountain jet.

The raider neared with incredible speed. Its rays were both slanted astern at a sharp angle, so that it slid forward with tremendous momentum.

The ship was operating two disintegrator rays, though only in a casual, intermittent fashion. But whenever they flashed downward with blinding brilliancy, forest, rocks and ground melted instantaneously into nothing, where they played upon them.

When later I inspected the scars left by these rays I found them some five feet deep and thirty feet wide, the exposed surfaces being lava-like in texture, but of a pale, iridescent, greenish hue.

No systematic use of the rays was made by the ship, however, until it reached a point over the center of the valley—the center of the community's activities. There it came to a sudden stop by shooting its repellor beams sharply forward and easing them back gradually to the vertical, holding the ship floating and motionless. Then the work of destruction began systematically.

Back and forth traveled the destroying rays, ploughing parallel furrows from hillside to hillside. We gasped in dismay, Wilma and I, as time after time we saw it plough through sections where we knew camps or plants were located.

"This is awful," she moaned, a terrified question in her eyes. "How could they know the location so exactly, Tony? Did you see? They were never in doubt. They stalled at a predetermined spot—and—and it was exactly the right spot."

We did not talk of what might happen if the rays were turned in our direction. We both knew. We would simply disintegrate in a split second into mere scattered electronic vibrations. Strangely enough, it was this self-reliant girl of the 25th Century, who clung to me, a relatively primitive man of the 20th, less familiar than she with the thought of this terrifying possibility, for moral support.

We knew that many of our companions must have been whisked into absolute non-existence before our eyes in these few moments. The whole thing paralyzed us into mental and physical immobility for I do not know how long.

It couldn't have been long, however, for the rays had not ploughed more than thirty of their twenty-foot furrows or so across the valley, when I regained control of myself, and brought Wilma to herself by shaking her roughly.

"How far will this rocket gun shoot, Wilma?" I demanded, drawing my pistol.

"It depends on your rocket, Tony. It will take even the longest range rocket, but you could shoot more accurately from a longer tube. But why? You couldn't penetrate the shell of that ship with rocket force, even if you could reach it."

I fumbled clumsily with my rocket pouch, for I was excited. I had an idea I wanted to try; a "hunch" I called it, forgetting that Wilma could not understand my ancient slang. But finally, with her help, I selected the longest range explosive rocket in my pouch, and fitted it to my pistol.

"It won't carry seven thousand feet, Tony," Wilma objected. But I took aim carefully. It was another thought that I had in my mind. The supporting repellor ray, I had been told, became molecular in character at what was called a logarithmic level of five (below that it was a purely electronic "flow" or pulsation between the source of the "carrier" and the average mass of the earth). Below that level if I could project my explosive bullet into this stream where it began to carry material substance upward, might it not rise with the air column, gathering speed and hitting the ship with enough impact to carry it through the shell? It was worth trying anyhow. Wilma became greatly excited, too, when she grasped the nature of my inspiration.

Feverishly I looked around for some formation of branches against which I could rest the pistol, for I had to aim most carefully. At last I found one. Patiently I sighted on the hulk of the ship far above us, aiming at the far side of it, at such an angle as would, so far as I could estimate, bring my bullet path through the forward repellor beam. At last the sights wavered across the point I sought and I pressed the button gently.

For a moment we gazed breathlessly.

Suddenly the ship swung bow down, as on a pivot, and swayed like a pendulum. Wilma screamed in her excitement.

"Oh, Tony, you hit it! You hit it! Do it again; bring it down!"

We had only one more rocket of extreme range between us, and we dropped it three times in our excitement in inserting it in my gun. Then, forcing myself to be calm by sheer will power, while Wilma stuffed her little fist into her mouth to keep from shrieking, I sighted carefully again and fired. In a flash, Wilma had grasped the hope that this discovery of mine might lead to the end of the Han domination.

The elapsed time of the rocket's invisible flight seemed an age.

Then we saw the ship falling. It seemed to plunge lazily, but actually it fell with terrific acceleration, turning end over end, its disintegrator rays, out of control, describing vast, wild arcs, and once cutting a gash through the forest less than two hundred feet from where we stood.

The crash with which the heavy craft hit the ground reverberated from the hills—the momentum of eighteen or twenty thousand tons, in a sheer drop of seven thousand feet. A mangled mass of metal, it buried itself in the ground, with poetic justice, in the middle of the smoking, semi-molten field of destruction it had been so deliberately ploughing.

The silence, the vacuity of the landscape, was oppressive, as the last echoes died away.

Then far down the hillside, a single figure leaped exultantly above the foliage screen. And in the distance another, and another.

In a moment the sky was punctured by signal rockets. One after another the little red puffs became drifting clouds.

"Scatter! Scatter!" Wilma exclaimed. "In half an hour there'll be an entire Han fleet here from Nu-yok, and another from Bah-flo. They'll get this instantly on their recordographs and location finders. They'll blast the whole valley and the country for miles beyond. Come, Tony. There's no time for the gang to rally. See the signals. We've got to jump. Oh, I'm so proud of you!"

Over the ridge we went, in long leaps toward the east, the country of the Delawares.

From time to time signal rockets puffed in the sky. Most of them were the "red warnings," the "scatter" signals. But from certain of the others, which Wilma identified as Wyoming rockets, she gathered that whoever was in command (we did not know whether the Boss was alive or not) was ordering an ultimate rally toward the south, and so we changed our course.

It was a great pity, I thought, that the clan had not been equipped throughout its membership with ultrophones, but Wilma explained to me, that not enough of these had been built for distribution as yet, although general distribution had been contemplated within a couple of months.

We traveled far before nightfall overtook us, trying only to put as much distance as possible between ourselves and the valley.

When gathering dusk made jumping too dangerous, we sought a comfortable spot beneath the trees, and consumed part of our emergency rations. It was the first time I had tasted the stuff—a highly nutritive synthetic substance called "concentro," which was, however, a bit bitter and unpalatable. But as only a mouthful or so was needed, it did not matter.

Neither of us had a cloak, but we were both thoroughly tired and happy, so we curled up together for warmth. I remember Wilma making some sleepy remark about our mating, as she cuddled up, as though the matter were all settled, and my surprise at my own instant acceptance of the idea, for I had not consciously thought of her that way before. But we both fell asleep at once.

In the morning we found little time for love making. The practical problem facing us was too great. Wilma felt that the Wyoming plan must be to rally in the Susquanna territory, but she had her doubts about the wisdom of this plan. In my elation at my success in bringing down the Han ship, and my newly found interest in my charming companion, who was, from my viewpoint of another century, at once more highly civilized and yet more primitive than myself, I had forgotten the ominous fact that the Han ship I had destroyed must have known the exact location of the Wyoming Works.

This meant, to Wilma's logical mind, either that the Hans had perfected new instruments as yet unknown to us, or that somewhere, among the Wyomings or some other nearby gang, there were traitors so degraded as to commit that unthinkable act of trafficking in information with the Hans. In either contingency, she argued, other Han raids would follow, and since the Susquannas had a highly developed organization and more than usually productive plants, the next raid might be expected to strike them.

But at any rate it was clearly our business to get in touch with the other fugitives as quickly as possible, so in spite of muscles that were sore from the excessive leaping of the day before, we continued on our way.

We traveled for only a couple of hours when we saw a multi-colored rocket in the sky, some ten miles ahead of us.

"Bear to the left, Tony," Wilma said, "and listen for the whistle."

"Why?" I asked.

"Haven't they given you the rocket code yet?" she replied. "That's what the green, followed by yellow and purple means; to concentrate five miles east of the rocket position. You know the rocket position itself might draw a play of disintegrator beams."

It did not take us long to reach the neighborhood of the indicated rallying, though we were now traveling beneath the trees, with but an occasional leap to a top branch to see if any more rocket smoke was floating above. And soon we heard a distant whistle.

We found about half the Gang already there, in a spot where the trees met high above a little stream. The Big Boss and Raid Bosses were busy reorganizing the remnants.

We reported to Boss Hart at once. He was silent, but interested, when he heard our story.

"You two stick close to me," he said, adding grimly, "I'm going back to the valley at once with a hundred picked men, and I'll need you."

Chapter V.

Setting the Trap

Inside of fifteen minutes we were on our way. A certain amount of caution was sacrificed for the sake of speed, and the men leaped away either across the forest top, or over open spaces of ground, but concentration was forbidden. The Big Boss named the spot on the hillside as the rallying point.

"We'll have to take a chance on being seen, so long as we don't group," he declared, "at least until within five miles of the rallying spot. From then on I want every man to disappear from sight and to travel under cover. And keep your ultrophones open, and tuned on ten-four-seven-six."

Wilma and I had received our battle equipment from the Gear boss. It consisted of a long-gun, a hand-gun, with a special case of ammunition constructed of inertron, which made the load weigh but a few ounces, and a short sword. This gear we strapped over each other's shoulders, on top of our jumping belts. In addition, we each received an ultrophone, and a light inertron blanket rolled into a cylinder about six inches long by two or three in diameter. This fabric was exceedingly thin and light, but it had considerable warmth, because of the mixture of inertron in its composition.

The Han raider neared with incredible speed. Its rays were both slanted astern at a sharp angle, so that it slid forward with tremendous momentum.... Whenever the disintegrator rays flashed downward with blinding brilliancy, forest, rocks and ground melted instantaneously into nothing, where they played upon them.

"This looks like business," Wilma remarked to me with sparkling eyes. (And I might mention a curious thing here. The word "business" had survived from the 20th Century American vocabulary, but not with any meaning of "industry" or "trade," for such things being purely community activities were spoken of as "work" and "clearing." Business simply meant fighting, and that was all.)

"Did you bring all this equipment from the valley?" I asked the Gear Boss.

The Han raider neared with incredible speed. Its rays were both slanted astern at a sharp angle, so that it slid forward with tremendous momentum.... Whenever the disintegrator rays flashed downward with blinding brilliancy, forest, rocks and ground melted instantaneously into nothing, where they played upon them.

"No," he said. "There was no time to gather anything. All this stuff we cleared from the Susquannas a few hours ago. I was with the Boss on the way down, and he had me jump on ahead and arrange it. But you two had better be moving. He's beckoning you now."

Hart was about to call us on our phones when we looked up. As soon as we did so, he leaped away, waving us to follow closely.

He was a powerful man, and he darted ahead in long, swift, low leaps up the banks of the stream, which followed a fairly straight course at this point. By extending ourselves, however, Wilma and I were able to catch up to him.

As we gradually synchronized our leaps with his, he outlined to us, between the grunts that accompanied each leap, his plan of action.

"We have to start the big business—unh—sooner or later," he said. "And if—unh—the Hans have found any way of locating our positions—unh—it's time to start now, although the Council of Bosses—unh—had intended waiting a few years until enough rocket ships have been—unh—built. But no matter what the sacrifice—unh—we can't afford to let them get us on the run—unh—. We'll set a trap for the yellow devils in the—unh—valley if they come back for their wreckage—unh—and if they don't, we'll go rocketing for some of their liners—unh—on the Nu-yok, Clee-lan, Si-ka-ga course. We can use—unh—that idea of yours of shooting up the repellor—unh—beams. Want you to give us a demonstration."

With further admonition to follow him closely, he increased his pace, and Wilma and I were taxed to our utmost to keep up with him. It was only in ascending the slopes that my tougher muscles overbalanced his greater skill, and I was able to set the pace for him, as I had for Wilma.

We slept in greater comfort that night, under our inertron blankets, and were off with the dawn, leaping cautiously to the top of the ridge overlooking the valley which Wilma and I had left.

The Boss scanned the sky with his ultroscope, patiently taking some fifteen minutes to the task, and then swung his phone into use, calling the roll and giving the men their instructions.

His first order was for us all to slip our ear and chest discs into permanent position.

These ultrophones were quite different from the one used by Wilma's companion scout the day I saved her from the vicious attack of the bandit Gang. That one was contained entirely in a small pocket case. These, with which we were now equipped, consisted of a pair of ear discs, each a separate and self-contained receiving set. They slipped into little pockets over our ears in the fabric helmets we wore, and shut out virtually all extraneous sounds. The chest discs were likewise self-contained sending sets, strapped to the chest a few inches below the neck and actuated by the vibrations from the vocal cords through the body tissues. The total range of these sets was about eighteen miles. Reception was remarkably clear, quite free from the static that so marked the 20th Century radios, and of a strength in direct proportion to the distance of the speaker.

The Boss' set was triple powered, so that his orders would cut in on any local conversations, which were indulged in, however, with great restraint, and only for the purpose of maintaining contacts.

I marveled at the efficiency of this modern method of battle communication in contrast to the clumsy signaling devices of more ancient times; and also at other military contrasts in which the 20th and 25th Century methods were the reverse of each other in efficiency. These modern Americans, for instance, knew little of hand to hand fighting, and nothing, naturally, of trench warfare. Of barrages they were quite ignorant, although they possessed weapons of terrific power. And until my recent flash of inspiration, no one among them, apparently, had ever thought of the scheme of shooting a rocket into a repellor beam and letting the beam itself hurl it upward into the most vital part of the Han ship.

Hart patiently placed his men, first giving his instructions to the campmasters, and then remaining silent, while they placed the individuals.

In the end, the hundred men were ringed about the valley, on the hillsides and tops, each in a position from which he had a good view of the wreckage of the Han ship. But not a man had come in view, so far as I could see, in the whole process.

The Boss explained to me that it was his idea that he, Wilma and I should investigate the wreck. If Han ships should appear in the sky, we would leap for the hillsides.

I suggested to him to have the men set up their long-guns trained on an imaginary circle surrounding the wreck. He busied himself with this after the three of us leaped down to the Han ship, serving as a target himself, while he called on the men individually to aim their pieces and lock them in position.

In the meantime Wilma and I climbed into the wreckage, but did not find much. Practically all of the instruments and machinery had been twisted out of all recognizable shape, or utterly destroyed by the ship's disintegrator rays which apparently had continued to operate in the midst of its warped remains for some moments after the crash.

It was unpleasant work searching the mangled bodies of the crew. But it had to be done. The Han clothing, I observed, was quite different from that of the Americans, and in many respects more like the garb to which I had been accustomed in the earlier part of my life. It was made of synthetic fabrics like silks, loose and comfortable trousers of knee length, and sleeveless shirts.

No protection, except that against drafts, was needed, Wilma explained to me, for the Han cities were entirely enclosed, with splendid arrangements for ventilation and heating. These arrangements of course were equally adequate in their airships. The Hans, indeed, had quite a distaste for unshaded daylight, since their lighting apparatus diffused a controlled amount of violet rays, making the unmodified sunlight unnecessary for health, and undesirable for comfort. Since the Hans did not have the secret of inertron, none of them wore anti-gravity belts. Yet in spite of the fact that they had to bear their own full weights at all times, they were physically far inferior to the Americans, for they lived lives of degenerative physical inertia, having machinery of every description for the performance of all labor, and convenient conveyances for any movement of more than a few steps.

Even from the twisted wreckage of this ship I could see that seats, chairs and couches played an extremely important part in their scheme of existence.

But none of the bodies were overweight. They seemed to have been the bodies of men in good health, but muscularly much underdeveloped. Wilma explained to me that they had mastered the science of gland control, and of course dietetics, to the point where men and women among them not uncommonly reached the age of a hundred years with arteries and general health in splendid condition.

I did not have time to study the ship and its contents as carefully as I would have liked, however. Time pressed, and it was our business to discover some clue to the deadly accuracy with which the ship had spotted the Wyoming Works.

The Boss had hardly finished his arrangements for the ring barrage, when one of the scouts on an eminence to the north, announced the approach of seven Han ships, spread out in a great semi-circle.

Hart leaped for the hillside, calling to us to do likewise, but Wilma and I had raised the flaps of our helmets and switched off our "speakers" for conversation between ourselves, and by the time we discovered what had happened, the ships were clearly visible, so fast were they approaching.

"Jump!" we heard the Boss order, "Deering to the north. Rogers to the east."

But Wilma looked at me meaningly and pointed to where the twisted plates of the ship, projecting from the ground, offered a shelter.

"Too late, Boss," she said. "They'd see us. Besides I think there's something here we ought to look at. It's probably their magnetic graph."

"You're signing your death warrant," Hart warned.

"We'll risk it," said Wilma and I together.

"Good for you," replied the Boss. "Take command then, Rogers, for the present. Do you all know his voice, boys?"

A chorus of assent rang in our ears, and I began to do some fast thinking as the girl and I ducked into the twisted mass of metal.

"Wilma, hunt for that record," I said, knowing that by the simple process of talking I could keep the entire command continuously informed as to the situation. "On the hillsides, keep your guns trained on the circles and stand by. On the hilltops, how many of you are there? Speak in rotation from Bald Knob around to the east, north, west."

In turn the men called their names. There were twenty of them.

I assigned them by name to cover the various Han ships, numbering the latter from left to right.

"Train your rockets on their repellor rays about three-quarters of the way up, between ships and ground. Aim is more important than elevation. Follow those rays with your aim continuously. Shoot when

I tell you, not before. Deering has the record. The Hans probably have not seen us, or at least think there are but two of us in the valley, since they're settling without opening up disintegrators. Any opinions?"

My ear discs remained silent.

"Deering and I remain here until they land and debark. Stand by and keep alert."

Rapidly and easily the largest of the Han ships settled to the earth. Three scouted sharply to the south, rising to a higher level. The others floated motionless about a thousand feet above.

Peeping through a small fissure between two plates, I saw the vast hulk of the ship come to rest full on the line of our prospective ring barrage. A door clanged open a couple of feet from the ground, and one by one the crew emerged.

Chapter VI.

The "Wyoming Massacre"

THEY'RE coming out of the ship." I spoke quietly, with my hand over my mouth, for fear they might hear me. "One—two—three—four, five—six—seven—eight—nine. That seems to be all. Who knows how many men a ship like that is likely to carry?"

"About ten, if there are no passengers," replied one of my men, probably one of those on the hillside.

"How are they armed?" I asked.

"Just knives," came the reply. "They never permit hand-rays on the ships. Afraid of accidents. Have a ruling against it."

"Leave them to us then," I said, for I had a hastily formed plan in my mind. "You, on the hillsides, take the ships above. Abandon the ring target. Divide up in training on those repellor rays. You, on the hilltops, all train on the repellors of the ships to the south. Shoot at the word, but not before.

"Wilma, crawl over to your left where you can make a straight leap for the door in that ship. These men are all walking around the wreck in a bunch. When they're on the far side, I'll give the word and you leap through that door in one bound. I'll follow. Maybe we won't be seen. We'll overpower the guard inside, but don't shoot. We may escape being seen by both this crew and ships above. They can't see over this wreck."

It was so easy that it seemed too good to be true. The Hans who had emerged from the ship walked round the wreckage lazily, talking in guttural tones, keenly interested in the wreck, but quite unsuspicious.

At last they were on the far side. In a moment they would be picking their way into the wreck.

"Wilma, leap!" I almost whispered the order.

The distance between Wilma's hiding place and the door in the side of the Han ship was not more than fifteen feet. She was already crouched with her feet braced against a metal beam. Taking the lift of that wonderful inertron belt into her calculation, she dove headforemost, like a green projectile, through the door. I followed in a split second, more clumsily, but no less speedily, bruising my shoulder painfully, as I ricocheted from the edge of the opening and brought up sliding against the unconscious girl; for she evidently had hit her head against the partition within the ship into which she had crashed.

We had made some noise within the ship. Shuffling footsteps were approaching down a well lit gangway.

"Any signs we have been observed?" I asked my men on the hillsides.

"Not yet," I heard the Boss reply. "Ships overhead still standing. No beams have been broken out. Men on ground absorbed in wreck. Most of them have crawled into it out of sight."

"Good," I said quickly. "Deering hit her head. Knocked out. One or more members of the crew approaching. We're not discovered yet. I'll take care of them. Stand a bit longer, but be ready."

I think my last words must have been heard by the man who was approaching, for he stopped suddenly.

I crouched at the far side of the compartment, motionless. I would not draw my sword if there were only one of them. He would be a weakling, I figured, and I should easily overcome him with my bare hands.

Apparently reassured at the absence of any further sound, a man came around a sort of bulkhead—and I leaped.

I swung my legs up in front of me as I did so, catching him full in the stomach and knocked him cold.

I ran forward along the keel gangway, searching for the control room. I found it well up in the nose of the ship. And it was deserted. What could I do to jam the controls of the ships that would not register on the recording instruments of the other ships? I gazed at the mass of controls. Levers and wheels galore. In the center of the compartment, on a massively braced universal joint mounting, was what I took for the repellor generator. A dial on it glowed and a faint hum came from within its shielding metallic case. But I had no time to study it.

Above all else, I was afraid that some automatic telephone apparatus existed in the room, through which I might be heard on the other ships. The risk of trying to jam the controls was too great. I abandoned the idea and withdrew softly. I would have to take a chance that there was no other member of the crew aboard.

I ran back to the entrance compartment. Wilma still lay where she had slumped down. I heard the voices of the Hans approaching. It was time to act. The next few seconds would tell whether the ships in the air would try or be able to melt us into nothingness. I spoke.

"Are you boys all ready?" I asked, creeping to a position opposite the door and drawing my hand-gun.

Again there was a chorus of assent.

"Then on the count of three, shoot up those repellor rays—all of them—and for God's sake, don't miss." And I counted.

I think my "three" was a bit weak. I know it took all the courage I had to utter it.

For an agonizing instant nothing happened, except that the landing party from the ship strolled into my range of vision.

Then startled, they turned their eyes upward. For an instant they stood frozen with horror at whatever they saw.

One hurled his knife at me. It grazed my cheek. Then a couple of them made a break for the doorway. The rest followed. But I fired pointblank with my hand-gun, pressing the button as fast as I could and aiming at their feet to make sure my explosive rockets would make contact and do their work.

The detonations of my rockets were deafening. The spot on which the Hans stood flashed into a blinding glare. Then there was nothing there except their torn and mutilated corpses. They had been fairly bunched, and I got them all.

I ran to the door, expecting any instant to be hurled into infinity by the sweep of a disintegrator ray.

Some eighth of a mile away I saw one of the ships crash to earth. A disintegrator ray came into my line of vision, wavered uncertainly for a moment and then began to sweep directly toward the ship in which I stood. But it never reached it. Suddenly, like a light switched off, it shot to one side, and a moment later another vast hulk crashed to earth. I looked out, then stepped out on the ground.

The only Han ships in the sky were two of the scouts to the south which were hanging perpendicularly, and sagging slowly down. The others must have crashed down while I was deafened by the sound of the explosion of my own rockets.

Somebody hit the other repellor ray of one of the two remaining ships and it fell out of sight beyond a hilltop. The other, farther away, drifted down diagonally, its disintegrator ray playing viciously over the ground below it.

I shouted with exultation and relief.

"Take back the command, Boss!" I yelled.

His commands, sending out jumpers in pursuit of the descending ship, rang in my ears, but I paid no attention to them. I leaped back into the compartment of the Han ship and knelt beside my Wilma. Her padded helmet had absorbed much of the blow, I thought; otherwise, her skull might have been fractured.

"Oh, my head!" she groaned, coming to as I lifted her gently in my arms and strode out in the open with her. "We must have won, dearest, did we?"

"We most certainly did," I reassured her. "All but one crashed and that one is drifting down toward the south; we've captured this one we're in intact. There was only one member of the crew aboard when we dove in."

As the American leaped, he swung his legs up in front of him, catching the Han full in the stomach.

Less than an hour afterward the Big Boss ordered the outfit to tune in ultrophones on three-twenty-three to pick up a translated broadcast of the Han intelligence office in Nu-yok from the Susquanna station. It was in the form of a public warning and news item, and read as follows:

"This is Public Intelligence Office, Nu-yok, broadcasting warning to navigators of private ships, and news of public interest. The squadron of seven ships, which left Nu-yok this morning to investigate the recent destruction of the GK-984 in the Wyoming Valley, has been destroyed by a series of mysterious explosions similar to those which wrecked the GK-984.

As the American leaped, he swung his legs up in front of him, catching the Han full in the stomach.

"The phones, viewplates, and all other signaling devices of five of the seven ships ceased operating suddenly at approximately the same moment, about seven-four-nine." (According to the Han system of reckoning time, seven and forty-nine one hundredths after midnight.) "After violent disturbances the location finders went out of operation. Electroactivity registers applied to the territory of the Wyoming Valley remain dead.

"The Intelligence Office has no indication of the kind of disaster which overtook the squadron except certain evidences of explosive phenomena similar to those in the case of the GK-984, which recently went dead while beaming the valley in a systematic effort to wipe out the works and camps of the tribesmen. The Office considers, as obvious, the deduction that the tribesmen have developed a new, and as yet undetermined, technique of attack on airships, and has recommended to the Heaven-Born that immediate and unlimited authority be given the Navigation Intelligence Division to make an investigation of this technique and develop a defense against it.

"In the meantime it urges that private navigators avoid this territory in particular, and in general hold as closely as possible to the official inter-city routes, which now are being patrolled by the entire force of the Military Office, which is beaming the routes generously to a width of ten miles. The Military Office reports that it is at present considering no retaliatory raids against the tribesmen. With the Navigation Intelligence Division, it holds that unless further evidence of the nature of the disaster is developed in the near future, the public interest will be better served, and at smaller cost of life, by a scientific research than by attempts at retaliation, which may bring destruction on all ships engaging therein. So unless further evidence actually is developed, or the Heaven-Born orders to the contrary, the Military will hold to a defensive policy.

"Unofficial intimations from Lo-Tan are to the effect that the Heaven-Council has the matter under consideration.

"The Navigation Intelligence Office permits the broadcast of the following condensation of its detailed observations:

"The squadron proceeded to a position above the Wyoming Valley where the wreck of the GK-984 was known to be, from the record of its location finder before it went dead recently. There the bottom projectoscope relays of all ships registered the wreck of the GK-984. Teleprojectoscope views of the wreck and the bowl of the valley showed no evidence of the presence of tribesmen. Neither ship registers nor base registers showed any indication of electroactivity except from the squadron itself. On orders from the Base Squadron Commander, the LD-248, LK-745 and LG-25 scouted southward at 3,000 feet. The GK-43, GK-981 and GK-220 stood above at 2,500 feet, and the GK-18 landed to permit personal inspection of the wreck by the science committee. The party debarked, leaving one man on board in the control cabin. He set all projectoscopes at universal focus except RB-3," (this meant the third projectoscope from the bow of the ship, on the right-hand side of the lower deck) "with which he followed the landing group as it walked around the wreck.

"The first abnormal phenomenon recorded by any of the instruments at Base was that relayed automatically from projectoscope RB-4 of the GK-18, which as the party disappeared from view in back of the wreck, recorded two green missiles of roughly cylindrical shape, projected from the wreckage into the landing compartment of the ship. At such close range these were not clearly defined, owing to the universal focus at which the projectoscope was set. The Base Captain of GK-18 at once ordered the man in the control room to investigate, and saw him leave the control room in compliance with this order. An instant later confused sounds reached the control-room electrophone, such as might be made by a man falling heavily, and footsteps reapproached the control room, a figure entering and leaving the control room hurriedly. The Base Captain now believes, and the stills of the photorecord support his belief, that this was not the crew member who had been left in the control room. Before the Base Captain could speak to him he left the room, nor was any response given to the attention signal the Captain flashed throughout the ship.

"At this point projectoscope RB-3 of the ship now out of focus control, dimly showed the landing party walking back toward the ship. RB-4 showed it more clearly. Then on both these instruments, a number of blinding explosives in rapid succession were seen and the electrophone relays registered terrific concussions; the ship's electronic apparatus and projectoscopes apparatus went dead.

"Reports of the other ships' Base Observers and Executives, backed by the photorecords, show the explosions as taking place in the midst of the landing party as it returned, evidently unsuspicious, to the ship. Then in rapid succession they indicate that terrific explosions occurred inside and outside the three ships standing above close to their rep-ray generators, and all signals from these ships thereupon went dead.

"Of the three ships scouting to the south, the LD-248 suffered an identical fate, at the same moment. Its records add little to the knowledge of the disaster. But with the LK-745 and the LG-25 it was different.

"The relay instruments of the LK-745 indicated the destruction by an explosion of the rear rep-ray generator, and that the ship hung stern down for a short space, swinging like a pendulum. The forward viewplates and indicators did not cease functioning, but their records are chaotic, except for one projectoscope still, which shows the bowl of the valley, and the GK-981 falling, but no visible evidence of tribesmen. The control-room viewplate is also a chaotic record of the ship's crew tumbling and falling to the rear wall. Then the forward rep-ray generator exploded, and all signals went dead.

"The fate of the LG-25 was somewhat similar, except that this ship hung nose down, and drifted on the wind southward as it slowly descended out of control.

"As its control room was shattered, verbal report from its Action Captain was precluded. The record of the interior rear viewplate shows members of the crew climbing toward the rear rep-ray generator in an attempt to establish manual control of it, and increase the lift. The projectoscope relays, swinging in wide arcs, recorded little of value except at the ends of their swings. One of these, from a machine which happened to be set in telescopic focus, shows several views of great value in picturing the falls of the other ships, and all of the rear projectoscope records enable the reconstruction in detail of the pendulum and torsional movements of the ship, and its sag toward the earth. But none of the views showing the forest below contain any indication of tribesmen's presence. A final explosion put this ship out of commission at a height of 1,000 feet, and at a point four miles S. by E. of the center of the valley."

The message ended with a repetition of the warning to other airmen to avoid the valley.

Chapter VII.

Incredible Treason

AFTER receiving this report, and reassurances of support from the Big Bosses of the neighboring Gangs, Hart determined to reestablish the Wyoming Valley community.

A careful survey of the territory showed that it was only the northern sections and slopes that had been "beamed" by the first Han ship.

The synthetic-fabrics plant had been partially wiped out, though the lower levels underground had not been reached by the dis ray. The forest screen above it, however, had been annihilated, and it was determined to abandon it, after removing all usable machinery and evidences of the processes that might be of interest to the Han scientists, should they return to the valley in the future.

The ammunition plant, and the rocket-ship plant, which had just been about to start operation at the time of the raid, were intact, as were the other important plants.

Hart brought the Camboss up from the Susquanna Works, and laid out new camp locations, scattering them farther to the south, and avoiding ground which had been seared by the Han beams and the immediate locations of the Han wrecks.

During this period, a sharp check was kept upon Han messages, for the phone plant had been one of the first to be put in operation, and when it became evident that the Hans did not intend any immediate reprisals, the entire membership of the community was summoned back, and normal life was resumed.

Wilma and I had been married the day after the destruction of the ships, and spent this intervening period in a delightful honeymoon, camping high in the mountains. On our return, we had a camp of our own, of course. We were assigned to location 1017. And as might be expected, we had a great deal of banter over which one of us was Camp Boss. The title stood after my name on the Big Boss' records, and those of the Big Camboss, of course, but Wilma airily held that this meant nothing at all—and generally succeeded in making me admit it whenever she chose.

I found myself a full-fledged member of the Gang now, for I had elected to search no farther for a permanent alliance, much as I would have liked to familiarize myself with this 25th Century life in other sections of the country. The Wyomings had a high morale, and had prospered under the rule of Big Boss Hart for many years. But many of the gangs, I found, were badly organized, lacked strong hands in authority, and were rife with intrigue. On the whole, I thought I would be wise to stay with a group which had already proved its friendliness, and in which I seemed to have prospects of advancement. Under these modern social and economic conditions, the kind of individual freedom to which I had been accustomed in the 20th Century was impossible. I would have been as much of a nonentity in every phase of human relationship by attempting to avoid alliances, as any man of the 20th Century would have been politically, who aligned himself with no political party.

This entire modern life, it appeared to me, judging from my ancient viewpoint, was organized along what I called "political" lines. And in this connection, it amused me to notice how universal had become the use of the word "boss." The leader, the person in charge or authority over anything, was a "boss." There was as little formality in his relations with his followers as there was in the case of the 20th Century political boss, and the same high respect paid him by his followers as well as the same high consideration by him of their interests. He was just as much of an autocrat, and just as much dependent upon the general popularity of his actions for the ability to maintain his autocracy.

The sub-boss who could not command the loyalty of his followers was as quickly deposed, either by them or by his superiors, as the ancient ward leader of the 20th Century who lost control of his votes.

As society was organized in the 20th Century, I do not believe the system could have worked in anything but politics. I tremble to think what would have happened, had the attempt been made to handle the A. E. F. this way during the First World War, instead of by that rigid military discipline and complete assumption of the individual as a mere standardized cog in the machine.

But owing to the centuries of desperate suffering the people had endured at the hands of the Hans, there developed a spirit of self-sacrifice and consideration for the common good that made the scheme applicable and efficient in all forms of human co-operation.

I have a little heresy about all this, however. My associates regard the thought with as much horror as many worthy people of the 20th Century felt in regard to any heretical suggestion that the original outline of government as laid down in the First Constitution did not apply as well to 20th Century conditions as to those of the early 19th.

In later years, I felt that there was a certain softening of moral fiber among the people, since the Hans had been finally destroyed with all their works; and Americans have developed a new luxury economy. I have seen signs of the reawakening of greed, of selfishness. The eternal cycle seems to be at work. I fear that slowly, though surely, private wealth is reappearing, codes of inflexibility are developing; they will be followed by corruption, degradation; and in the end some cataclysmic event will end this era and usher in a new one.

All this, however, is wandering afar from my story, which concerns our early battles against the Hans, and not our more modern problems of self-control.

Our victory over the seven Han ships had set the country ablaze. The secret had been carefully communicated to the other gangs, and the country was agog from one end to the other. There was feverish activity in the ammunition plants, and the hunting of stray Han ships became an enthusiastic sport. The results were disastrous to our hereditary enemies.

From the Pacific Coast came the report of a great transpacific liner of 75,000 tons "lift" being brought to earth from a position of invisibility above the clouds. A dozen Sacramentos had caught the hazy outlines of its rep rays approaching them, head-on, in the twilight, like ghostly pillars reaching into the sky. They had fired rockets into it with ease, whereas they would have had difficulty in hitting it if it had been moving at right angles to their position. They got one rep ray. The other was not strong enough to hold it up. It floated to earth, nose down, and since it was unarmed and unarmored, they had no difficulty in shooting it to pieces and massacring its crew and passengers. It seemed barbarous to me. But then I did not have centuries of bitter persecution in my blood.

From the Jersey Beaches we received news of the destruction of a Nu-yok-A-lan-a liner. The Sand-snipers, practically invisible in their sand-colored clothing, and half buried along the beaches, lay in wait for days, risking the play of dis beams along the route, and finally registering four hits within a week. The Hans discontinued their service along this route, and as evidence that they were badly shaken by our success, sent no raiders down the Beaches.

It was a few weeks later that Big Boss Hart sent for me.

"Tony," he said, "There are two things I want to talk to you about. One of them will become public property in a few days, I think. We aren't going to get any more Han ships by shooting up their repellor rays unless we use much larger rockets. They are wise to us now. They're putting armor of great thickness in the hulls of their ships below the rep-ray machines. Near Bah-flo this morning a party of Eries shot one without success. The explosions staggered her, but did not penetrate. As near as we can gather from their reports, their laboratories have developed a new alloy of great tensile strength and elasticity which nevertheless lets the rep rays through like a sieve. Our reports indicate that the Eries' rockets bounced off harmlessly. Most of the party was wiped out as the dis rays went into action on them.

"This is going to mean real business for all of the gangs before long. The Big Bosses have just held a national ultrophone council. It was decided that America must organize on a national basis. The first move is to develop sectional organization by Zones. I have been made Superboss of the Mid-Atlantic Zone.

"We're in for it now. The Hans are sure to launch reprisal expeditions. If we're to save the race we must keep them away from our camps and plants. I'm thinking of developing a permanent field force, along the lines of the regular armies of the 20th Century you told me about. Its business will be twofold: to carry the warfare as much as possible to the Hans, and to serve as a decoy, to keep their attention from our plants. I'm going to need your help in this.

"The other thing I wanted to talk to you about is this: Amazing and impossible as it seems, there is a group, or perhaps an entire gang, somewhere among us, that is betraying us to the Hans. It may be the Bad Bloods, or it may be one of those gangs who live near one of the Han cities. You know, a hundred and fifteen or twenty years ago there were certain of these people's ancestors who actually degraded themselves by mating with the Hans, sometimes even serving them as slaves, in the days before they brought all their service machinery to perfection.

"There is such a gang, called the Nagras, up near Bah-flo, and another in Mid-Jersey that men call the Pineys. But I hardly suspect the Pineys. There is little intelligence among them. They wouldn't have the information to give the Hans, nor would they be capable of imparting it. They're absolute savages."

"Just what evidence is there that anybody has been clearing information to the Hans?" I asked.

"Well," he replied, "first of all there was that raid upon us. That first Han ship knew the location of our plants exactly. You remember it floated directly into position above the valley and began a systematic beaming. Then, the Hans quite obviously have learned that we are picking up their electrophone waves, for they've gone back to their old, but extremely accurate, system of directional control. But we've been getting them for the past week by installing automatic re-broadcast units along the scar paths. This is what the Americans called those strips of country directly under the regular ship routes of the Hans, who as a matter of precaution frequently blasted them with their dis beams to prevent the growth of foliage which might give shelter to the Americans. But they've been beaming those paths so hard, it looks as though they even had information of this strategy. And in addition, they've been using code. Finally, we've picked up three of their messages in which they discuss, with some nervousness, the existence of our 'mysterious' ultrophone."

"But they still have no knowledge of the nature and control of ultronic activity?" I asked.

"No," said the Big Boss thoughtfully, "they don't seem to have a bit of information about it."

"Then it's quite clear," I ventured, "that whoever is 'clearing' us to them is doing it piecemeal. It sounds like a bit of occasional barter, rather than an out-and-out alliance. They're holding back as much information as possible for future bartering, perhaps."

"Yes," Hart said, "and it isn't information the Hans are giving in return, but some form of goods, or privilege. The trick would be to locate the goods. I guess I'll have to make a personal trip around among the Big Bosses."

Chapter VIII.

The Han City

THIS conversation set me thinking. All of the Han electrophone inter-communication had been an open record to the Americans for a good many years, and the Hans were just finding it out. For centuries they had not regarded us as any sort of a menace. Unquestionably it had never occurred to them to secrete their own records. Somewhere in Nu-yok or Bah-flo, or possibly in Lo-Tan itself, the record of this traitorous transaction would be more or less openly filed. If we could only get at it! I wondered if a raid might not be possible.

Bill Hearn and I talked it over with our Han-affairs Boss and his experts. There ensued several days of research, in which the Han records of the entire decade were scanned and analyzed. In the end they picked out a mass of detail, and fitted it together into a very definite picture of the great central filing office of the Hans in Nu-yok, where the entire mass of official records was kept, constantly available for instant projectoscoping to any of the city's offices, and of the system by which the information was filed.

The attempt began to look feasible, though Hart instantly turned the idea down when I first presented it to him. It was unthinkable, he said. Sheer suicide. But in the end I persuaded him.

"I will need," I said, "Blash, who is thoroughly familiar with the Han library system; Bert Gaunt, who for years has specialized on their military offices; Bill Barker, the ray specialist, and the best swooper pilot we have." Swoopers are one-man and two-man ships, developed by the Americans, with skeleton backbones of inertron (during the war painted green for invisibility against the green forests below) and "bellies" of clear ultron.

"That will be Mort Gibbons," said Hart. "We've only got three swoopers left, Tony, but I'll risk one of them if you and the others will voluntarily risk your existences. But mind, I won't urge or order one of you to go. I'll spread the word to every Plant Boss at once to give you anything and everything you need in the way of equipment."

When I told Wilma of the plan, I expected her to raise violent and tearful objections, but she didn't. She was made of far sterner stuff than the women of the 20th Century. Not that she couldn't weep as copiously or be just as whimsical on occasion; but she wouldn't weep for the same reasons.

She just gave me an unfathomable look, in which there seemed to be a bit of pride, and asked eagerly for the details. I confess I was somewhat disappointed that she could so courageously risk my loss, even though I was amazed at her fortitude. But later I was to learn how little I knew her then.

We were ready to slide off at dawn the next morning. I had kissed Wilma good-bye at our camp, and after a final conference over our plans, we boarded our craft and gently glided away over the tree tops on a course, which, after crossing three routes of the Han ships, would take us out over the Atlantic, off the Jersey coast, whence we would come up on Nu-yok from the ocean.

Twice we had to nose down and lie motionless on the ground near a route while Han ships passed. Those were tense moments. Had the green back of our ship been observed, we would have been disintegrated in a second. But it wasn't.

Once over the water, however, we climbed in a great spiral, ten miles in diameter, until our altimeter registered ten miles. Here Gibbons shut off his rocket motor, and we floated, far above the level of the Atlantic liners, whose course was well to the north of us anyhow, and waited for nightfall.

Then Gibbons turned from his control long enough to grin at me.

"I have a surprise for you, Tony," he said, throwing back the lid of what I had supposed was a big supply case. And with a sigh of relief, Wilma stepped out of the case.

"If you 'go into zero' (a common expression of the day for being annihilated by the disintegrator ray), you don't think I'm going to let you go alone, do you, Tony? I couldn't believe my ears last night when you spoke of going without me, until I realized that you are still five hundred years behind the times in lots of ways. Don't you know, dear heart, that you offered me the greatest insult a husband could give a wife? You didn't, of course."

The others, it seemed, had all been in on the secret, and now they would have kidded me unmercifully, except that Wilma's eyes blazed dangerously.

At nightfall, we maneuvered to a position directly above the city. This took some time and calculation on the part of Bill Barker, who explained to me that he had to determine our point by ultronic bearings. The slightest resort to an electronic instrument, he feared, might be detected by our enemies' locators. In fact, we did not dare bring our swooper any lower than five miles for fear that its capacity might be reflected in their instruments.

Finally, however, he succeeded in locating above the central tower of the city.

"If my calculations are as much as ten feet off," he remarked with confidence, "I'll eat the tower. Now the rest is up to you, Mort. See what you can do to hold her steady. No—here, watch this indicator—the red beam, not the green one. See—if you keep it exactly centered on the needle, you're O.K. The width of the beam represents seventeen feet. The tower platform is fifty feet square, so we've got a good margin to work on."

For several moments we watched as Gibbons bent over his levers, constantly adjusting them with deft touches of his fingers. After a bit of wavering, the beam remained centered on the needle.

"Now," I said, "let's drop."

I opened the trap and looked down, but quickly shut it again when I felt the air rushing out of the ship into the rarefied atmosphere in a torrent. Gibbons literally yelled a protest from his instrument board.

"I forgot," I mumbled. "Silly of me. Of course, we'll have to drop out of compartment."

The compartment, to which I referred, was similar to those in some of the 20th Century submarines. We all entered it. There was barely room for us to stand, shoulder to shoulder. With some struggles, we got into our special air helmets and adjusted the pressure. At our signal, Gibbons exhausted the air in the compartment, pumping it into the body of the ship, and as the little signal light flashed, Wilma threw open the hatch.

Setting the ultron-wire reel, I climbed through, and began to slide down gently.

We all had our belts on, of course, adjusted to a weight balance of but a few ounces. And the five-mile reel of ultron wire that was to be our guide, was of gossamer fineness, though, anyway, I believe it would have lifted the full weight of the five of us, so strong and tough was this invisible metal. As an extra precaution, since the wire was of the purest metal, and therefore totally invisible, even in daylight, we all had our belts hooked on small rings that slid down the wire.

I went down with the end of the wire. Wilma followed a few feet above me, then Barker, Gaunt and Blash. Gibbons, of course, stayed behind to hold the ship in position and control the paying out of the line. We all had our ultrophones in place inside our air helmets, and so could converse with one another and with Gibbons. But at Wilma's suggestion, although we would have liked to let the Big Boss listen in, we kept them adjusted to short-range work, for fear that those who had been clearing with the Hans, and against whom we were on a raid for evidence, might also pick up our conversation. We had no fear that the Hans would hear us. In fact, we had the added advantage that, even after we landed, we could converse freely without danger of their hearing our voices through our air helmets.

For a while I could see nothing below but utter darkness. Then I realized, from the feel of the air as much as from anything, that we were sinking through a cloud layer. We passed through two more cloud layers before anything was visible to us.

Then there came under my gaze, about two miles below, one of the most beautiful sights I have ever seen; the soft, yet brilliant, radiance of the great Han city of Nu-yok. Every foot of its structural members seemed to glow with a wonderful incandescence, tower piled up on tower, and all built on the vast base-mass of the city, which, so I had been told, sheered upward from the surface of the rivers to a height of 728 levels.

The city, I noticed with some surprise, did not cover anything like the same area as the New York of the 20th Century. It occupied, as a matter of fact, only the lower half of Manhattan Island, with one section straddling the East River, and spreading out sufficiently over what once had been Brooklyn, to provide berths for the great liners and other air craft.

Straight beneath my feet was a tiny dark patch. It seemed the only spot in the entire city that was not aflame with radiance. This was the central tower, in the top floors of which were housed the vast library of record files and the main projectoscope plant.

"You can shoot the wire now," I ultrophoned Gibbons, and let go the little weighted knob. It dropped like a plummet, and we followed with considerable speed, but braking our descent with gloved hands sufficiently to see whether the knob, on which a faint light glowed as a signal for ourselves, might be observed by any Han guard or night prowler. Apparently it was not, and we again shot down with accelerated speed.

We landed on the roof of the tower without any mishap, and fortunately for our plan, in darkness. Since there was nothing above it on which it would have been worth while to shed illumination, or from which there was any need to observe it, the Hans had neglected to light the tower roof, or indeed to occupy it at all. This was the reason we had selected it as our landing place.

As soon as Gibbons had our word, he extinguished the knob light, and the knob, as well as the wire, became totally invisible. At our ultrophoned word, he would light it again.

"No gun play now," I warned. "Swords only, and then only if absolutely necessary."

Closely bunched, and treading as lightly as only inertron-belted people could, we made our way cautiously through a door and down an inclined plane to the floor below, where Gaunt and Blash assured us the military offices were located.

Twice Barker cautioned us to stop as we were about to pass in front of mirror-like "windows" in the passage wall, and flattening ourselves to the floor, we crawled past them.

"Projectoscopes," he said. "Probably on automatic record only, at this time of night. Still, we don't want to leave any records for them to study after we're gone."

"Were you ever here before?" I asked.

"No," he replied, "but I haven't been studying their electrophone communications for seven years without being able to recognize these machines when I run across them."

Chapter IX.

The Fight in the Tower

SO far we had not laid eyes on a Han. The tower seemed deserted. Blash and Gaunt, however, assured me that there would be at least one man on "duty" in the military offices, though he would probably be asleep, and two or three in the library proper and the projectoscope plant.

"We've got to put them out of commission," I said. "Did you bring the 'dope' cans, Wilma?"

"Yes," she said, "two for each. Here," and she distributed them.

We were now two levels below the roof, and at the point where we were to separate.

I did not want to let Wilma out of my sight, but it was necessary.

According to our plan, Barker was to make his way to the projectoscope plant, Blash and I to the library, and Wilma and Gaunt to the military office.

Blash and I traversed a long corridor, and paused at the great arched doorway of the library. Cautiously we peered in. Seated at three great switchboards were library operatives. Occasionally one of them would reach lazily for a lever, or sleepily push a button, as little numbered lights winked on and off. They were answering calls for electrograph and viewplate records on all sorts of subjects from all sections of the city.

I apprised my companions of the situation.

"Better wait a bit," Blash added. "The calls will lessen shortly."

Wilma reported an officer in the military office sound asleep.

"Give him the can, then," I said.

Barker was to do nothing more than keep watch in the projectoscope plant, and a few moments later he reported himself well concealed, with a splendid view of the floor.

"I think we can take a chance now," Blash said to me, and at my nod, he opened the lid of his dope can. Of course, the fumes did not affect us, through our helmets. They were absolutely without odor or visibility, and in a few seconds the librarians were unconscious. We stepped into the room.

There ensued considerable cautious observation and experiment on the part of Gaunt, working from the military office, and Blash in the library; while Wilma and I, with drawn swords and sharply attuned microphones, stood guard, and occasionally patrolled nearby corridors.

"I hear something approaching," Wilma said after a bit, with excitement in her voice. "It's a soft, gliding sound."

"That's an elevator somewhere," Barker cut in from the projectoscope floor. "Can you locate it? I can't hear it."

"It's to the east of me," she replied.

"And to my west," said I, faintly catching it. "It's between us, Wilma, and nearer you than me. Be careful. Have you got any information yet, Blash and Gaunt?"

"Getting it now," one of them replied. "Give us two minutes more."

"Keep at it then," I said. "We'll guard."

The soft, gliding sound ceased.

"I think it's very close to me," Wilma almost whispered. "Come closer, Tony. I have a feeling something is going to happen. I've never known my nerves to get taut like this without reason."

In some alarm, I launched myself down the corridor in a great leap toward the intersection whence I knew I could see her.

In the middle of my leap my ultrophone registered her gasp of alarm. The next instant I glided to a stop at the intersection to see Wilma backing toward the door of the military office, her sword red with blood, and an inert form on the corridor floor. Two other Hans were circling to either side of her with wicked-looking knives, while a third evidently a high officer, judging by the resplendence of his garb tugged desperately to get an electrophone instrument out of a bulky pocket. If he ever gave the alarm, there was no telling what might happen to us.

I was at least seventy feet away, but I crouched low and sprang with every bit of strength in my legs. It would be more correct to say that I dived, for I reached the fellow head on, with no attempt to draw my legs beneath me.

Some instinct must have warned him, for he turned suddenly as I hurtled close to him. But by this time I had sunk close to the floor, and had stiffened myself rigidly, lest a dragging knee or foot might just prevent my reaching him. I brought my blade upward and over. It was a vicious slash that laid him open, bisecting him from groin to chin, and his dead body toppled down on me, as I slid to a tangled stop.

The other two startled, turned. Wilma leaped at one and struck him down with a side slash. I looked up at this instant, and the dazed fear on his face at the length of her leap registered vividly. The Hans knew nothing of our inertron belts, it seemed, and these leaps and dives of ours filled them with terror.

As I rose to my feet, a gory mess, Wilma, with a poise and speed which I found time to admire even in this crisis, again leaped. This time she dove head first as I had done and, with a beautifully executed thrust, ran the last Han through the throat.

Uncertainly, she scrambled to her feet, staggered queerly, and then sank gently prone on the corridor. She had fainted.

At this juncture, Blash and Gaunt reported with elation that they had the record we wanted.

"Back to the roof, everybody!" I ordered, as I picked Wilma up in my arms. With her inertron belt, she felt as light as a feather.

Gaunt joined me at once from the military office, and at the intersection of the corridor, we came upon Blash waiting for us. Barker, however, was not in evidence.

"Where are you, Barker?" I called.

"Go ahead," he replied. "I'll be with you on the roof at once."

We came out in the open without any further mishap, and I instructed Gibbons in the ship to light the knob on the end of the ultron wire. It flashed dully a few feet away from us. Just how he had maneuvered the ship to keep our end of the line in position, without its swinging in a tremendous arc, I have never been able to understand. Had not the night been an unusually still one, he could not have checked the initial pendulum-like movements. As it was, there was considerable air current at certain of the levels, and in different directions too. But Gibbons was an expert of rare ability and sensitivity in the handling of a rocket ship, and he managed, with the aid of his delicate instruments, to sense the drifts almost before they affected the fine ultron wire, and to neutralize them with little shifts in the position of the ship.

Blash and Gaunt fastened their rings to the wire, and I hooked my own and Wilma's on, too. But on looking around, I found Barker was still missing.

"Barker, come!" I called. "We're waiting."

"Coming!" he replied, and indeed, at that instant, his figure appeared up the ramp. He chuckled as he fastened his ring to the wire, and said something about a little surprise he had left for the Hans.

"Don't reel in the wire more than a few hundred feet," I instructed Gibbons. "It will take too long to wind it in. We'll float up, and when we're aboard, we can drop it."

In order to float up, we had to dispense with a pound or two of weight apiece. We hurled our swords from us, and kicked off our shoes as Gibbons reeled up the line a bit, and then letting go of the wire, began to hum upward on our rings with increasing velocity.

The rush of air brought Wilma to, and I hastily explained to her that we had been successful. Receding far below us now, I could see our dully shining knob swinging to and fro in an ever widening arc, as it crossed and recrossed the black square of the tower roof. As an extra precaution, I ordered Gibbons to shut off the light, and to show one from the belly of the ship, for so great was our speed now, that I began to fear we would have difficulty in checking ourselves. We were literally falling upward, and with terrific acceleration.

Fortunately, we had several minutes in which to solve this difficulty, which none of us, strangely enough, had foreseen. It was Gibbons who found the answer.

"You'll be all right if all of you grab the wire tight when I give the word," he said. "First I'll start reeling it in at full speed. You won't get much of a jar, and then I'll decrease its speed again gradually, and its weight will hold you back. Are you ready? One—two—three!"

We all grabbed tightly with our gloved hands as he gave the word. We must have been rising a good bit faster than he figured, however, for it wrenched our arms considerably, and the maneuver set up a sickening pendulum motion.

For a while all we could do was swing there in an arc that may have been a quarter of a mile across, about three and a half miles above the city, and still more than a mile from our ship.

Gibbons skilfully took up the slack as our momentum pulled up the line. Then at last we had ourselves under control again, and continued our upward journey, checking our speed somewhat with our gloves.

There was not one of us who did not breathe a big sigh of relief when we scrambled through the hatch safely into the ship again, cast off the ultron line and slammed the trap shut.

Little realizing that we had a still more terrible experience to go through, we discussed the information Blash and Gaunt had between them extracted from the Han records, and the advisability of ultrophoning Hart at once.

Chapter X.

The Walls of Hell

THE traitors were, it seemed, a degenerate gang of Americans, located a few miles north of Nu-yok on the wooded banks of the Hudson, the Sinsings. They had exchanged scraps of information to the Hans in return for several old repellor-ray machines, and the privilege of tuning in on the Han electronic power broadcast for their operation, provided their ships agreed to subject themselves to the orders of the Han traffic office, while aloft.

The rest wanted to ultrophone their news at once, since there was always danger that we might never get back to the gang with it.

I objected, however. The Sinsings would be likely to pick up our message. Even if we used the directional projector, they might have scouts out to the west and south in the big inter-gang stretches of country. They would flee to Nu-yok and escape the punishment they merited. It seemed to be vitally important that they should not, for the sake of example to other weak groups among the American gangs, as well as to prevent a crisis in which they might clear more vital information to the enemy.

"Out to sea again," I ordered Gibbons. "They'll be less likely to look for us in that direction."

"Easy, Boss, easy," he replied. "Wait until we get up a mile or two more. They must have discovered evidences of our raid by now, and their dis-ray wall may go in operation any moment."

Even as he spoke, the ship lurched downward and to one side.

"There it is!" he shouted. "Hang on, everybody. We're going to nose straight up!" And he flipped the rocket-motor control wide open.

Looking through one of the rear ports, I could see a nebulous, luminous ring, and on all sides the atmosphere took on a faint iridescence.

We were almost over the destructive range of the disintegrator-ray wall, a hollow cylinder of annihilation shooting upward from a solid ring of generators surrounding the city. It was the main defense system of the Hans, which had never been used except in periodic tests. They may or may not have suspected that an American rocket ship was within the cylinder; probably they had turned on their generators more as a precaution to prevent any reaching a position above the city.

But even at our present great height, we were in great danger. It was a question how much we might have been harmed by the rays themselves, for their effective range was not much more than seven or eight miles. The greater danger lay in the terrific downward rush of air within the cylinder to replace that which was being burned into nothingness by the continual play of the disintegrators. The air fell into the cylinder with the force of a gale. It would be rushing toward the wall from the outside with terrific force also, but, naturally, the effect was intensified on the interior.

Our ship vibrated and trembled. We had only one chance of escape—to fight our way well above the current. To drift down with it meant ultimately, and inevitably, to be sucked into the destruction wall at some lower level.

But very gradually and jerkily our upward movement, as shown on the indicators, began to increase, and after an hour of desperate struggle we were free of the maelstrom and into the rarefied upper levels. The terror beneath us was now invisible through several layers of cloud formations.

Gibbons brought the ship back to an even keel, and drove her eastward into one of the most brilliantly gorgeous sunrises I have ever seen.

We described a great circle to the south and west, in a long easy dive, for he had cut out his rocket motors to save them as much as possible. We had drawn terrifically on their fuel reserves in our battle with the elements. For the moment, the atmosphere below cleared, and we could see the Jersey coast far beneath, like a great map.

"We're not through yet," remarked Gibbons suddenly, pointing at his periscope, and adjusting it to telescopic focus. "A Han ship, and a 'drop ship' at that—and he's seen us. If he whips that beam of his on us, we're done."

I gazed, fascinated, at the viewplate. What I saw was a cigar-shaped ship not dissimilar to our own in design, and from the proportional size of its ports, of about the same size as our swoopers. We learned later that they carried crews, for the most part of not more than three or four men. They had streamline hulls and tails that embodied universal-jointed double fish-tail rudders. In operation they rose to great heights on their powerful repellor rays, then gathered speed either by a straight nose dive, or an inclined dive in which they sometimes used the repellor ray slanted at a sharp angle. He was already above us, though several miles to the north. He could, of course, try to get on our tail and "spear" us with his beam as he dropped at us from a great height.

Suddenly his beam blazed forth in a blinding flash, whipping downward slowly to our right. He went through a peculiar corkscrew-like evolution, evidently maneuvering to bring his beam to bear on us with a spiral motion.

Gibbons instantly sent our ship into a series of evolutions that must have looked like those of a frightened hen. Alternately, he used the forward and the reverse rocket blasts, and in varying degree. We fluttered, we shot suddenly to right and left, and dropped like a plummet in uncertain movements. But all the time the Han scout dropped toward us, determinedly whipping the air around us with his beam. Once it sliced across beneath us, not more than a hundred feet, and we dropped with a jar into the pocket formed by the destruction of the air.

He had dropped to within a mile of us, and was coming with the speed of a projectile, when the end came. Gibbons always swore it was sheer luck. Maybe it was, but I like pilots who are lucky that way.

In the midst of a dizzy, fluttering maneuver of our own, with the Han ship enlarging to our gaze with terrifying rapidity, and its beam slowly slicing toward us in what looked like certain destruction within the second, I saw Gibbons' fingers flick at the lever of his rocket gun and a split second later the Han ship flew apart like a clay pigeon.

We staggered, and fluttered crazily for several moments while Gibbons struggled to bring our ship into balance, and a section of about four square feet in the side of the ship near the stern slowly crumbled like rusted metal. His beam actually had touched us, but our explosive rocket had got him a thousandth of a second sooner.

Part of our rudder had been annihilated, and our motor damaged. But we were able to swoop gently back across Jersey, fortunately crossing the ship lanes without sighting any more Han craft, and finally settling to rest in the little glade beneath the trees, near Hart's camp.

Chapter XI.

The New Boss

WE had ultrophoned our arrival and the Big Boss himself, surrounded by the Council, was on hand to welcome us and learn our news. In turn we were informed that during the night a band of raiding Bad Bloods, disguised under the insignia of the Altoonas, a gang some distance to the west of us, had destroyed several of our camps before our people had rallied and driven them off. Their purpose, evidently, had been to embroil us with the Altoonas, but fortunately, one of our exchanges recognized the Bad Blood leader, who had been slain.

The Big Boss had mobilized the full raiding force of the Gang, and was on the point of heading an expedition for the extermination of the Bad Bloods.

I looked around the grim circle of the sub-bosses, and realized the fate of America, at this moment, lay in their hands. Their temper demanded the immediate expenditure of our full effort in revenging ourselves for this raid. But the strategic exigencies, to my mind, quite clearly demanded the instant and absolute extermination of the Sinsings. It might be only a matter of hours, for all we knew, before these degraded people would barter clues to the American ultronic secrets to the Hans.

"How large a force have we?" I asked Hart.

"Every man and maid who can be spared," he replied. "That gives us seven hundred married and unmarried men, and three hundred girls, more than the entire Bad Blood Gang. Every one is equipped with belts, ultrophones, rocket guns and swords, and all fighting mad."

I meditated how I might put the matter to these determined men, and was vaguely conscious that they were awaiting my words.

Finally I began to speak. I do not remember to this day just what I said. I talked calmly, with due regard for their passion, but with deep conviction. I went over the information we had collected, point by point, building my case logically, and painting a lurid picture of the danger impending in that half-alliance between the Sinsings and the Hans of Nu-yok. I became impassioned, culminating, I believe, with a vow to proceed single-handed against the hereditary enemies of our race, "if the Wyomings were blindly set on placing a gang feud ahead of honor and duty and the hopes of all America."

As I concluded, a great calm came over me, as of one detached. I had felt much the same way during several crises in the First World War. I gazed from face to face, striving to read their expressions, and in a mood to make good my threat without any further heroics, if the decision was against me.

But it was Hart who sensed the temper of the Council more quickly than I did, and looked beyond it into the future.

He arose from the tree trunk on which he had been sitting.

"That settles it," he said, looking around the ring. "I have felt this thing coming on for some time now. I'm sure the Council agrees with me that there is among us a man more capable than I, to boss the Wyoming Gang, despite his handicap of having had all too short a time in which to familiarize himself with our modern ways and facilities. Whatever I can do to support his effective leadership, at any cost, I pledge myself to do."

As he concluded, he advanced to where I stood, and taking from his head the green-crested helmet that constituted his badge of office, to my surprise he placed it in my mechanically extended hand.

The roar of approval that went up from the Council members left me dazed. Somebody ultrophoned the news to the rest of the Gang, and even though the earflaps of my helmet were turned up, I could hear the cheers with which my invisible followers greeted me, from near and distant hillsides, camps and plants.

My first move was to make sure that the Phone Boss, in communicating this news to the members of the Gang, had not re-broadcast my talk nor mentioned my plan of shifting the attack from the Bad Bloods to the Sinsings. I was relieved by his assurance that he had not, for it would have wrecked the whole plan. Everything depended upon our ability to surprise the Sinsings.

So I pledged the Council and my companions to secrecy, and allowed it to be believed that we were about to take to the air and the trees against the Bad Bloods.

That outfit must have been badly scared, the way they were "burning" the ether with ultrophone alibis and propaganda for the benefit of the more distant gangs. It was their old game, and the only method by which they had avoided extermination long ago from their immediate neighbors—these appeals to the spirit of American brotherhood, addressed to gangs too far away to have had the sort of experience with them that had fallen to our lot.

I chuckled. Here was another good reason for the shift in my plans. Were we actually to undertake the exterminations of the Bad Bloods at once, it would have been a hard job to convince some of the gangs that we had not been precipitate and unjustified. Jealousies and prejudices existed. There were gangs which would give the benefit of the doubt to the Bad Bloods, rather than to ourselves, and the issue was now hopelessly beclouded with the clever lies that were being broadcast in an unceasing stream.

But the extermination of the Sinsings would be another thing. In the first place, there would be no warning of our action until it was all over, I hoped. In the second place, we would have indisputable proof, in the form of their rep-ray ships and other paraphernalia, of their traffic with the Hans; and the state of American prejudice, at the time of which I write held trafficking with the Hans a far more heinous thing than even a vicious gang feud.

I called an executive session of the Council at once. I wanted to inventory our military resources.

I created a new office on the spot, that of "Control Boss," and appointed Ned Garlin to the post, turning over his former responsibility as Plants Boss to his assistant. I needed someone, I felt, to tie in the records of the various functional activities of the campaign, and take over from me the task of keeping the records of them up to the minute.

I received reports from the bosses of the ultrophone unit, and those of food, transportation, fighting gear, chemistry, electronic activity and electrophone intelligence, ultroscopes, air patrol and contact guard.

My ideas for the campaign, of course, were somewhat tinged with my 20th Century experience, and I found myself faced with the task of working out a staff organization that was a composite of the best and most easily applied principles of business and military efficiency, as I knew them from the viewpoint of immediate practicality.

What I wanted was an organization that would be specialized, functionally, not as that indicated above, but from the angles of: intelligence as to the Sinsings' activities; intelligence as to Han activities; perfection of communication with my own units; co-operation of field command; and perfect mobilization of emergency supplies and resources.

It took several hours of hard work with the Council to map out the plan. First we assigned functional experts and equipment to each "Division" in accordance with its needs. Then these in turn were reassigned by the new Division Bosses to the Field Commands as needed, or as Independent or Headquarters Units. The two intelligence divisions were named the White and the Yellow, indicating that one specialized on the American enemy and the other on the Mongolians.

The division in charge of our own communications, the assignment of ultrophone frequencies and strengths, and the maintenance of operators and equipment, I called "Communications."

I named Bill Hearn to the post of Field Boss, in charge of the main or undetached fighting units, and to the Resources Division, I assigned all responsibility for what few aircraft we had; and all transportation and supply problems, I assigned to "Resources." The functional bosses stayed with this division.

We finally completed our organization with the assignment of liaison representatives among the various divisions as needed.

Thus I had a "Headquarters Staff" composed of the Division Bosses who reported directly to Ned Garlin as Control Boss, or to Wilma as my personal assistant. And each of the Division Bosses had a small staff of his own.

In the final summing up of our personnel and resources, I found we had roughly a thousand "troops," of whom some three hundred and fifty were, in what I called the Service Divisions, the rest being in Bill Hearn's Field Division. This latter number, however, was cut down somewhat by the assignment of numerous small units to detached service. Altogether, the actual available fighting force, I figured, would number about five hundred, by the time we actually went into action.

We had only six small swoopers, but I had an ingenious plan in my mind, as the result of our little raid on Nu-yok, that would make this sufficient, since the reserves of inertron blocks were larger than I expected to find them. The Resources Division, by packing its supply cases a bit tight, or by slipping in extra blocks of inertron, was able to reduce each to a weight of a few ounces. These easily could be floated and towed by the swoopers in any quantity. Hitched to ultron lines, it would be a virtual impossibility for them to break loose.

The entire personnel, of course, was supplied with jumpers, and if each man and girl was careful to adjust balances properly, the entire number could also be towed along through the air, grasping wires of ultron, swinging below the swoopers, or stringing out behind them.

There would be nothing tiring about this, because the strain would be no greater than that of carrying a one or two pound weight in the hand, except for air friction at high speeds. But to make doubly sure that we should lose none of our personnel, I gave strict orders that the belts and tow lines should be equipped with rings and hooks.

So great was the efficiency of the fundamental organization and discipline of the Gang, that we got under way at nightfall.

One by one the swoopers eased into the air, each followed by its long train or "kite-tail" of humanity and supply cases hanging lightly from its tow line. For convenience, the tow lines were made of an alloy of ultron which, unlike the metal itself, is visible.

At first these "tails" hung downward, but as the ships swung into formation and headed eastward toward the Bad Blood territory, gathering speed, they began to string out behind. And swinging low from each ship on heavily weighted lines, ultroscope, ultrophone, and straight-vision observers keenly scanned the countryside, while intelligence men in the swoopers above bent over their instrument boards and viewplates.

Leaving Control Boss Ned Garlin temporarily in charge of affairs,

Wilma and I dropped a weighted line from our ship, and slid down about half way to the under lookouts, that is to say, about a thousand feet. The sensation of floating swiftly through the air like this, in the absolute security of one's confidence in the inertron belt, was one of never-ending delight to me.

We reascended into the swooper as the expedition approached the territory of the Bad Bloods, and directed the preparations for the bombardment. It was part of my plan to appear to carry out the attack as originally planned.

About fifteen miles from their camps our ships came to a halt and maintained their positions for a while with the idling blasts of their rocket motors, to give the ultroscope operators a chance to make a thorough examination of the territory below us, for it was very important that this next step in our program should be carried out with all secrecy.

At length they reported the ground below us entirely clear of any appearance of human occupation, and a gun unit of long-range specialists was lowered with a dozen rocket guns, equipped with special automatic devices that the Resources Division had developed at my request, a few hours before our departure. These were aiming and timing devices. After calculating the range, elevation and rocket charges carefully, the guns were left, concealed in a ravine, and the men were hauled up into the ship again. At the predetermined hour, those unmanned rocket guns would begin automatically to bombard the Bad Bloods' hillsides, shifting their aim and elevation slightly with each shot, as did many of our artillery pieces in the First World War.

In the meantime, we turned south about twenty miles, and grounded, waiting for the bombardment to begin before we attempted to sneak across the Han ship lane. I was relying for security on the distraction that the bombardment might furnish the Han observers.

It was tense work waiting, but the affair went through as planned, our squadron drifting across the route high enough to enable the ships' tails of troops and supply cases to clear the ground.

In crossing the second ship route, out along the Beaches of Jersey, we were not so successful in escaping observation. A Han ship came speeding along at a very low elevation. We caught it on our electronic location and direction finders, and also located it with our ultroscopes, but it came so fast and so low that I thought it best to remain where we had grounded the second time, and lie quiet, rather than get under way and cross in front of it.

The point was this. While the Hans had no such devices as our ultroscopes, with which we could see in the dark (within certain limitations of course), and their electronic instruments would be virtually useless in uncovering our presence, since all but natural electronic activities were carefully eliminated from our apparatus, except electrophone receivers (which are not easily spotted), the Hans did have some very highly sensitive sound devices which operated with great efficiency in calm weather, so far as sounds emanating from the air were concerned. But the "ground roar" greatly confused their use of these instruments in the location of specific sounds floating up from the surface of the earth.

This ship must have caught some slight noise of ours, however, in its sensitive instruments, for we heard its electronic devices go into play, and picked up the routine report of the noise to its Base Ship Commander. But from the nature of the conversation, I judged they had not identified it, and were, in fact, more curious about the detonations they were picking up now from the Bad Blood lands some sixty miles or so to the west.

Immediately after this ship had shot by, we took the air again, and following much the same route that I had taken the previous night, climbed in a long semi-circle out over the ocean, swung toward the north and finally the west. We set our course, however, for the Sinsings' land north of Nu-yok, instead of for the city itself.

Chapter XII.

The Finger of Doom

AS we crossed the Hudson River, a few miles north of the city, we dropped several units of the Yellow Intelligence Division, with full instrumental equipment. Their apparatus cases were nicely balanced at only a few ounces weight each, and the men used their chute capes to ease their drops.

We recrossed the river a little distance above and began dropping White Intelligence units and a few long and short range gun units. Then we held our position until we began to get reports. Gradually we ringed the territory of the Sinsings, our observation units working busily and patiently at their locators and scopes, both aloft and aground, until Garlin finally turned to me with the remark:

"The map circle is complete now, Boss. We've got clear locations all the way around them."

"Let me see it," I replied, and studied the illuminated viewplate map, with its little overlapping circles of light that indicated spots proved clear of the enemy by ultroscopic observation.

I nodded to Bill Hearn. "Go ahead now, Hearn," I said, "and place your barrage men."

He spoke into his ultrophone, and three of the ships began to glide in a wide ring around the enemy territory. Every few seconds, at the word from his Unit Boss, a gunner would drop off the wire, and slipping the clasp of his chute cape, drift down into the darkness below.

Bill formed two lines, parallel to and facing the river, and enclosing the entire territory of the enemy between them. Above and below, straddling the river, were two defensive lines. These latter were merely to hold their positions. The others were to close in toward each other, pushing a high-explosive barrage five miles ahead of them. When the two barrages met, both lines were to switch to short-vision-range barrage and continue to close in on any of the enemy who might have drifted through the previous curtain of fire.

In the meantime Bill kept his reserves, a picked corps of a hundred men (the same that had accompanied Hart and myself in our fight with the Han squadron) in the air, divided about equally among the "kite-tails" of four ships.

A final roll call, by units, companies, divisions and functions, established the fact that all our forces were in position. No Han activity was reported, and no Han broadcasts indicated any suspicion of our expedition. Nor was there any indication that the Sinsings had any knowledge of the fate in store for them. The idling of rep-ray generators was reported from the center of their camp, obviously those of the ships the Hans had given them—the price of their treason to their race.

Again I gave the word, and Hearn passed on the order to his subordinates.

Far below us, and several miles to the right and left, the two barrage lines made their appearance. From the great height to which we had risen, they appeared like lines of brilliant, winking lights, and the detonations were muffled by the distances into a sort of rumbling, distant thunder. Hearn and his assistants were very busy: measuring, calculating, and snapping out ultrophone orders to unit commanders that resulted in the straightening of lines and the closing of gaps in the barrage.

The White Division Boss reported the utmost confusion in the Sinsing organization. They were, as might be expected, an inefficient, loosely disciplined gang, and repeated broadcasts for help to neighboring gangs. Ignoring the fact that the Mongolians had not used explosives for many generations, they nevertheless jumped at the conclusion that they were being raided by the Hans. Their frantic broadcasts persisted in this thought, despite the nervous electrophonic inquiries of the Hans themselves, to whom the sound of the battle was evidently audible, and who were trying to locate the trouble.

At this point, the swooper I had sent south toward the city went into action as a diversion, to keep the Hans at home. Its "kite-tail" loaded with long-range gunners, using the most highly explosive rockets we had, hung invisible in the darkness of the sky and bombarded the city from a distance of about five miles. With an entire city to shoot at, and the object of creating as much commotion therein as possible, regardless of actual damage, the gunners had no difficulty in hitting the mark. I could see the glow of the city and the stabbing flashes of exploding rockets. In the end, the Hans, uncertain as to what was going on, fell back on a defensive policy, and shot their "hell cylinder," or wall of upturned disintegrator rays into operation. That, of course, ended our bombardment of them. The rays were a perfect defense, disintegrating our rockets as they were reached.

If they had not sent out ships before turning on the rays, and if they had none within sufficient radius already in the air, all would be well.

I queried Garlin on this, but he assured me Yellow Intelligence reported no indications of Han ships nearer than 800 miles. This would probably give us a free hand for a while, since most of their instruments recorded only imperfectly or not at all, through the death wall.

Requisitioning one of the viewplates of the headquarters ship, and the services of an expert operator, I instructed him to focus on our lines below. I wanted a close-up of the men in action.

He began to manipulate his controls and chaotic shadows moved rapidly across the plate, fading in and out of focus, until he reached an adjustment that gave me a picture of the forest floor, apparently 100 feet wide, with the intervening branches and foliage of the trees appearing like shadows that melted into reality a few feet above the ground.

I watched one man setting up his long-gun with skillful speed. His lips pursed slightly as though he were whistling, as he adjusted the tall tripod on which the long tube was balanced. Swiftly he twirled the knobs controlling the aim and elevation of his piece. Then, lifting a belt of ammunition from the big box, which itself looked heavy enough to break down the spindly tripod, he inserted the end of it in the lock of his tube and touched the proper combination of buttons.

Then he stepped aside, and occupied himself with peering carefully through the trees ahead. Not even a tremor shook the tube, but I knew that at intervals of something less than a second, it was discharging small projectiles which, traveling under their own continuously reduced power, were arching into the air, to fall precisely five miles ahead and explode with the force of eight-inch shells, such as we used in the First World War.

Another gunner, fifty feet to the right of him, waved a hand and called out something to him. Then, picking up his own tube and tripod, he gauged the distance between the trees ahead of him, and the height of their lowest branches, and bending forward a bit, flexed his muscles and leaped lightly, some twenty-five feet. Another leap took him another twenty feet or so, where he began to set up his piece.

I ordered my observer then to switch to the barrage itself. He got a close focus on it, but this showed little except a continuous series of blinding flashes, which, from the viewplate, lit up the entire interior of the ship. An eight-hundred-foot focus proved better. I had thought that some of our French and American artillery of the 20th Century had achieved the ultimate in mathematical precision of fire, but I had never seen anything to equal the accuracy of that line of terrific explosions as it moved steadily forward, mowing down trees as a scythe cuts grass (or used to 500 years ago), literally churning up the earth and the splintered, blasted remains of the forest giants, to a depth of from ten to twenty feet.

By now the two curtains of fire were nearing each other, lines of vibrant, shimmering, continuous, brilliant destruction, inevitably squeezing the panic-stricken Sinsings between them.

Even as I watched, a group of them, who had been making a futile effort to get their three rep-ray machines into the air, abandoned their efforts, and rushed forth into the milling mob.

I queried the Control Boss sharply on the futility of this attempt of theirs, and learned that the Hans, apparently in doubt as to what was going on, had continued to "play safe," and broken off their power broadcast, after ordering all their own ships east of the Alleghenies to the ground, for fear these ships they had traded to the Sinsings might be used against them.

Again I turned to my viewplate, which was still focussed on the central section of the Sinsing works. The confusion of the traitors was entirely that of fear, for our barrage had not yet reached them.

Some of them set up their long-guns and fired at random over the barrage line, then gave it up. They realized that they had no target to shoot at, no way of knowing whether our gunners were a few hundred feet or several miles beyond it.

Their ultrophone men, of whom they did not have many, stood around in tense attitudes, their helmet phones strapped around their ears, nervously fingering the tuning controls at their belts. Unquestionably they must have located some of our frequencies, and overheard many of our reports and orders. But they were confused and disorganized. If they had an Ultrophone Boss they evidently were not reporting to him in an organized way.

They were beginning to draw back now before our advancing fire. With intermittent desperation, they began to shoot over our barrage again, and the explosions of their rockets flashed at widely scattered points beyond. A few took distance "pot shots."

Oddly enough it was our own forces that suffered the first casualties in the battle. Some of these distance shots by chance registered hits, while our men were under strict orders not to exceed their barrage distances.

Seen upon the ultroscope viewplate, the battle looked as though it were being fought in daylight, perhaps on a cloudy day, while the explosions of the rockets appeared as flashes of extra brilliance.

The two barrage lines were not more than five hundred feet apart when the Sinsings resorted to tactics we had not foreseen. We noticed first that they began to lighten themselves by throwing away extra equipment. A few of them in their excitement threw away too much, and shot suddenly into the air. Then a scattering few floated up gently, followed by increasing numbers, while still others, preserving a weight balance, jumped toward the closing barrages and leaped high, hoping to clear them. Some succeeded. We saw others blown about like leaves in a windstorm, to crumple and drift slowly down, or else to fall into the barrage, their belts blown from their bodies.

However, it was not part of our plan to allow a single one of them to escape and find his way to the Hans. I quickly passed the word to Bill Hearn to have the alternate men in his line raise their barrages and heard him bark out a mathematical formula to the Unit Bosses.

We backed off our ships as the explosions climbed into the air in stagger formation until they reached a height of three miles. I don't believe any of the Sinsings who tried to float away to freedom succeeded.

But we did know later, that a few who leaped the barrage got away and ultimately reached Nu-yok.

It was those who managed to jump the barrage who gave us the most trouble. With half of our long-guns turned aloft, I foresaw we would not have enough to establish successive ground barrages and so ordered the barrage back two miles, from which positions our "curtains" began to close in again, this time, however, gauged to explode, not on contact, but thirty feet in the air. This left little chance for the Sinsings to leap either over or under it.

Gradually, the two barrages approached each other until they finally met, and in the grey dawn the battle ended.

Our own casualties amounted to forty-seven men in the ground forces, eighteen of whom had been slain in hand to hand fighting with the few of the enemy who managed to reach our lines, and sixty-two in the crew and "kite-tail" force of swooper No. 4, which had been located by one of the enemy's ultroscopes and brought down with long-gun fire.

Since nearly every member of the Sinsing Gang had, so far as we knew, been killed, we considered the raid a great success.

It had, however, a far greater significance than this. To all of us who took part in the expedition, the effectiveness of our barrage tactics definitely established a confidence in our ability to overcome the Hans.

As I pointed out to Wilma:

"It has been my belief all along, dear, that the American explosive rocket is a far more efficient weapon than the disintegrator ray of the Hans, once we can train all our gangs to use it systematically and in co-ordinated fashion. As a weapon in the hands of a single individual, shooting at a mark in direct line of vision, the rocket-gun is inferior in destructive power to the dis ray, except as its range may be a little greater. The trouble is that to date it has been used only as we used our rifles and shot guns in the 20th Century. The possibilities of its use as artillery, in laying barrages that advance along the ground, or climb into the air, are tremendous.

"The dis ray inevitably reveals its source of emanation. The rocket gun does not. The dis ray can reach its target only in a straight line. The rocket may be made to travel in an arc, over intervening obstacles, to an unseen target.

"Nor must we forget that our ultronists now are promising us a perfect shield against the dis ray in inertron."

"I tremble though, Tony dear, when I think of the horrors that are ahead of us. The Hans are clever. They will develop defenses against our new tactics. And they are sure to mass against us not only the full force of their power in America, but the united forces of the World Empire. They are a cowardly race in one sense, but clever as the very Devils in Hell, and inheritors of a calm, ruthless, vicious persistency."

"Nevertheless," I prophesied, "the Finger of Doom points squarely at them today, and unless you and I are killed in the struggle, we shall live to see America blast the Yellow Blight from the face of the Earth."

THE END.